One Tragic June:

Based on actual letters and stories

Jean Pugh Shipman

One Tragic June

This is a work of fiction. The characters and events in this book are based on true family letters and stories, but some names and details have been changed for privacy.

ISBN (Ingram Paperback): 979-8-9933414-2-2

ISBN (eBook): 979-8-9933414-1-5

ISBN (Kindle Edition): 979-8-9933414-3-9

First Edition: 2025

Library of Congress Control Number: 2025921423

Library of Congress Cataloguing-in-Publication Data Requested.

This book is dedicated to my deceased sister, Patty. You taught me many important lessons in life, but mainly to strive to use the talent and abilities given to me to the maximum. I trust you know you are deeply missed and thought of constantly.

Preface
1964

"You do know what happened to her, don't you?"

Mother looks at her older cousin and replies, "She had an operation in New York City, got sick afterwards, and died." Silence.

The cousin, Marion, whispers, as I am nearby and in elementary school, "Let's discuss this more when we can"— nodding toward me.

This is how I learned about the death of their cousin.

Marion frequently babysat us, as she lived in our small town, and Mother needed her to care for us when she worked at a small community bank three buildings away. Marion was almost a member of our immediate family and a daily visitor, as she delivered our mail from the post office along with mail for nearby elderly women.

My curiosity was stoked. I was determined to learn more about this shared cousin whose name I didn't even know. In fact, I never knew there was a missing cousin; I had so many.

— ∞ —

My upbringing in a small rural town with no stop lights in the 1950s and 1960s had its benefits and its disadvantages. We were part of a village, desirous or not. People knew everything about us, and we knew all about them. Our modest house—the Pugh home—was in midtown with easy access to the town's key features—a family-owned and operated grocery store, a town hall, a post office, an elementary school, two churches of different denominations, and a bank. The other key ingredient to life in a small town is the other villagers. They influence one's knowledge of the world—they tell you about life in big cities, they share details about their aches and pains, and they encourage you to stay informed of community events and happenings—some prefer to call this gossip.

Gossip is indeed what I was raised on. We interpreted it as caring deeply about others, as we wanted to offer our help when it was needed. In a small rural community in the '50s, it was neighbors who prayed for your family when illness, disasters, or other life-threatening events happened. I recall, as a child, tripping on the sidewalk when running to the grocery store. A neighbor who lived in the house where I had fallen rescued me. Sitting me on her kitchen counter, she cleaned and bandaged the wound, soothed my nerves, and told me I was going to live. I could still get the needed items from the store.

Two major sources of entertainment in our town were family and church. I cannot tell you the number of picnics, weddings, funerals, reunions and graduations I attended as a child. When I wasn't participating in church activities—time was spent with cousins, aunts, uncles, and grandmothers. Both of my grandfathers passed before I was old enough to remember them well.

Hearing about an unknown cousin was scandalous and why this new secret was so juicy. There had to be more to this story. I thought I knew everything about my family. I had read tomes written by family members documenting our family trees and our ancestral lines. I couldn't fathom a missing link— an unidentified person in our tree. Why would such a person not be remembered or mentioned? Why would Mother's cousin die from an operation and no one care? Did she catch a deadly disease, tuberculosis perhaps, or a bad case of the flu? And if so, why wasn't this discussed? I had heard about everyone else's death, why not hers?

By the way, I'm Jean Pugh Shipman.

BOOK I

Chapter 1
Saying Goodbye—June 3, 1944
Reading, Pennsylvania

"June, you will go to New York City next week via bus and train. A man named Sam will meet you at the train station in New York and take you to your hotel."

While I heard these words, I could not focus on the implications of this trip. Going to New York City should have been exciting, I have never been far from my hometown and am downright scared. Who will talk to me or want to help me? Will anyone understand my situation, and if so, will they accept me? I feel so isolated and alone—yet I am going to one of the largest cities in the world. How will I manage walking into department stores I have only read about? How will I navigate a town with traffic signals? Will people make fun of me due to my Plain dress in a world where fashion rules? Why am I being forced to do this? Do my parents no longer love me? Why this directive? Am I the first person in the world to get myself into this situation? Surely not. Yet I have no one to turn to for help. Parents are to be obeyed, and I am obligated to do what they want. I am not of legal age yet, being 17 years and four months old. They can state what my future holds, and I have no recourse. Respect prevents me from arguing with them. All I can do is retreat and start to pack. I am going to New York City.

On Tuesday, Father takes me to a bus station in a large town near ours. He stands with me as we wait for the bus to arrive. I have never ridden a bus; I am jittery and on edge. My nerves are firing and I am shifting from foot to foot. Apprehension is my middle name, along with sad. I am leaving the only home I know to be among strangers. It is hard for me to understand why my parents are making me do this. They keep saying it is for my own good. I would be ridiculed if I stayed home, and my life would never be the same. While I share some of their concerns, I do not feel my life would end if I stayed on the farm. It would be different, but it would not end. I think about talking with Father while we are alone, but an announcement is made—my bus is arriving, and I need to say goodbye and get on it. Father carries my one duffel bag for me—I do not own a proper suitcase as travel is not part of my experience repertoire.

Father is quiet; no words are expressed. However, I see tears in his eyes as he hands the bag to the bus driver to load. He turns to me, and to my surprise, gives me a big hug. The first ever. Our family is stoic when it comes to displaying emotions; hugs and kisses are uncommon. I might get some from Mother, but never from Father. He is more upset than I have given him credit. Apparently, the decision to send me to New York City is not an easy one, as he has repeatedly told me. I wipe his fallen tears off his face with a hankie, board the bus, find a seat, and wave goodbye.

Chapter 2
All Aboard—June 3, 1944
Philadelphia, Pennsylvania

A couple of hours pass; the bus pulls into a train station in Philadelphia (Philly), Pennsylvania. Philly is another city I have read and heard about from others in my small town, but it is a new place for me. I exit the bus grabbing my duffel bag and enter the crowded train station. I follow the instructions Father gave me. "Look for a large board with train numbers and departure times. Your train number and the track it will arrive on will be listed. If all else fails, look for an information desk or someone who works for the railroad and ask for assistance. Do not be shy about getting help. It is not a weakness."

There are too many people for my comfort. How can I be surrounded by so many and yet feel so alone? Can I see a big announcement board? There is so much chatter from multiple conversations—people conversing with one another as if this is normal life—waiting for yet another train. Ho hum. Well, I am alert, and any sound makes me jump. I am a displaced country bumpkin, and yet, this is only a train station. Can I live with this kind of constant chaotic noise? Will I survive? Will I be a misfit wherever I go? I am frightened and excited simultaneously. It dawns on me this could be a new beginning.

I could find I like city living and might never return home. I have read stories of others who went missing only to be found in a large city where they had escaped to learn more about the world. Will I add to the statistics of these relocated individuals? Can I survive and select my own path through life? I have never ever had these thoughts—what is happening to me? I need to pray and ask God to forgive me for thinking of leaving my parents, siblings, and safe living environment. I am jostled out of these thoughts by a loud train whistle and a conductor yelling "All Aboard." I look for the train to New York City.

The announcement board Father had told me about is overhead, and I am amazed how many different trains are running. I had expected five or six, but there are well over 30 departures listed. I recall Father telling me to look for the train number, and indeed there it is, Number 19. It is the sixth entry, arriving on Track #6. The train will not depart for another 30 minutes, so I look around, find the gate, and move to sit on a bench near it. I will be okay. Take a deep breath. I am no longer a child, and after this experience, I will be justified in thinking so. I begin to calm down and breathe easier. I am feeling more like an adult, or at least what I think an adult would feel like.

I escape my musings and pay attention to others waiting for the train. Who are my fellow travelers and why are they traveling? Are they going to college, meeting a boyfriend or girlfriend, husband, or wife? Why pick today to travel and are they as apprehensive as I am, or are they seasoned travelers, and today is yet another train ride, one of many? I see a few families, but mostly men with briefcases, who probably are going to the city to conduct business. There is only one other single woman traveling. If I need to share a seat, should I sit beside her for safety? I wonder if she is travelling alone or with a companion who is off buying food for the ride. How do I know what seat I need to sit in? I forgot to ask Father about this aspect. Luckily, the ticket indicates a reserved seat—seat number 6B. Six is a lucky number for me; I take this as a good sign. If the train has two seats together, I will sit with whomever has seat 6A, I assume. Time will tell. I sure wish Peter was travelling with me.

Soon, the announcement for the train to New York City is made and people gather at the top of the gate. I grab my bag and do the same. I guess we do not have to arrange ourselves by our seat numbers, as everyone queues as they arrive. I descend the stairs and see two sets of tracks. Confused at first which track—to take, I quickly see they are numbered. I follow the crowd to Track 6 where Train #19 is to arrive. Soon, I hear a whistle and see the headlights of the approaching train. This is it, this is the beginning of a new journey for me. I board the

train, find my car and seat. There is a man in 6A. He is
oblivious to my Plain clothes—dark colors, black stockings,
and an off-white apron or bib over my dress—as I am wearing
my long shawl and have removed my head covering. My long
hair is wrapped in its usual bun, another signal of plainness. He
glances at me, but I do not return his look for fear of having to
speak to him. I place the duffel bag overhead, as I see others
do, sit and sigh. So far, so good. New York City, I am on my
way.

Chapter 3
I am Plain—June 1944

New York City is so different for me due to my background. I am Plain. I am referring to the term given to my religious beliefs and those of my family. We are not Amish, not Mennonite, but Church of the Brethren. All these religious sects are called the Anabaptists. I did not realize this until I took baptism classes to learn more about the church to become a member. One is not allowed to join the church until one is a teenager and has completed instructional classes. We are not forced to join, but if we do and decide later to leave the membership, we may be shunned by our families and others. I only interact with other people who are Plain, so I do not think twice about labeling myself as Plain. I am me; but no, I am Plain me.

We do not believe our bodies should be used to entice others and therefore dress plainly, without jewelry or lace. This style is how the label *Plain* originated—to describe our appearance. A set of rules and a way of living come with being Plain, called an Ordnung. In the sect's rules, cars are permitted if they are painted black (including bumpers), and we can accept rides in cars. We gather Sunday mornings for services at a small building, called a meetinghouse. We are taught the "golden rule" and abide by it daily. Many members of our Faith have large families with seven to eight children who help with farm chores and household labor.

It is a wholesome life and an isolating one. It is not hard to be Plain if you surround yourself with others of the Faith. It is hard to see others outside the Faith enjoy dancing, playing cards, and drinking though. It should not be according to our sermons, but it is tough for me. I read a lot and yearn to be accepted and able to take part in these activities. It seems like others are having more fun than I am, and they do not have to perform chores. Freedom from responsibilities is something I have yet to experience. To date, I have lived on a farm with my family in rural Pennsylvania. Let me offer some additional background about my life prior to New York City.

Chapter 4
Plain has its Limits—September 1938
Reading, Pennsylvania

"Come on," Mother says. "You will be late for your first day at the new school. Do you know what dress you want to wear? I will wake your brothers and see you downstairs in 15 minutes."

"Mother, thank you. I want to wear the new dark blue dress you made. I love it and want to remember you throughout the day." I am so excited to be going to a larger school with more students. The walk to this school will take about 20 minutes, as it is over a mile away in a small town.

To give you an idea of the exposure I have had to others to date, I have six siblings: three sisters and three brothers. Two brothers are older than me. I fall almost in the middle as far as birth order—as child number three. We live in a four-bedroom farmhouse. The boys share a large bedroom, as there are three of them. I share a room with my oldest sister, Mary. My other two sisters share a room as well. We were born over a 16-year timespan. Our parents love us, we know, but they are of the Plain Faith and do not express emotions. Hugging and kissing are not what we do, especially with strangers or others.

We are taught to be stoic and guarded. Our speech is formal, even among our immediate family members.

We are a vessel of God and need to conduct ourselves in a manner pleasing to God. We read the Bible in the morning as part of breakfast, and we are expected to read it when we get home and do a daily assignment related to our reading. We discuss this assignment briefly with our parents before we go to bed. The girls have a common assignment different from the boys. Father discusses the boys' assignment with them, and Mother does the same with the girls. This ritual does not occur of course on Sundays, as we attend services with fellow believers. I learn a lot from these discussions and services and feel I have a solid religious foundation for my life.

However, I desire to experience more. I do not feel religion is enough. I am exposed to the world through reading, by going to a library of sorts. A public library places a small selection of books to borrow at our local bank, which is about a half mile away from our home. New books arrive weekly. I read about 50 books a year. Reading makes me aware of things most members of the Plain membership have never explored. I consider myself well-informed but not experienced. I have yet to go to a big city or even a large town. I have never shopped in a department store nor opened a bank account. I save a small allowance in a tin container, giving most of it to the collection during Sunday services. I yearn to expand my horizons; yet, I do not know what to expect in return. I cannot wait to grow and experience life outside of the religious sect.

Chapter 5
School Life—September 1938

"Welcome class. I am Mr. Martin. It is great to have you join me for a year of classes and instruction. With me is Mr. Miller who will cover topics such as arithmetic and spelling. We want to begin today by having each of you introduce yourself—state your name, where you live, and a fact about yourself you want to share."

Panic sets in. I look around and count. There are 20 students in the room; eight of us are Plain and from nearby farms, with the other 12 being from nearby towns. The three-quarter-sleeved dark blue dress I am wearing made of homespun thread, the white apron or bib, and the covering on my head indicate plainness. My palms are sweating, as I am nervous about introducing myself. I have never spoken to a group this large and this mixed. The class has both boys and girls, the majority being boys. Sweat starts to form on my forehead, and my throat seems to swell. I luckily am not the first person to do an introduction. When the students look toward me, I feel my face flush, quickly turning beet red. I quietly offer "June" and state where I live.

There is dead silence. A student says "What did you say? We can't hear you!"

I speak again a little louder and repeat the information. Another student yells "What, cat have your tongue? Speak loudly or don't speak at all."

This time I shout and everyone in the room laughs. I want to die – to be anywhere but in this classroom. I bow my head and luckily, the student seated beside me gets the hint and offers his information. The first impression I make is less than positive; I become nicknamed "Silent Plain June" by my classmates. It is not a fond nickname; and unfortunately, it defines me for the rest of my school years.

Chapter 6
A Comrade—September 1938

"Are you okay?" asks the one boy student at recess. He talks to me while I am standing in the corner of the playground. I jump as I did not realize anyone was close by. I look into his caring eyes and say, "I am as good as I can be. I am embarrassed as I am not comfortable speaking with people outside of the family and meetinghouse." He reaches out his hand to shake mine; I do not accept. Girls are not to be forward with boys, and I thought this kind of contact would be frowned upon. But it pleases me.

"Do not worry," he says. "I could tell you were uncomfortable, and I am sorry our fellow classmates are rude. They should not make fun of your uneasiness. As you heard, I am Michael. I wanted to come over and let you know not everyone is making fun of you. Please do not let the labeling get to you. They will soon forget the 'Silent Plain June' nickname."

I sure hope so I think. Michael making this innuendo pleases me, as it helps me to forget about myself for the moment. We rejoin the other students. His kindness leaves a lasting favorable impression on me. He rescued me when no one else had.

When I get home, Mother asks me how my first day at the new school went. I sheepishly say, "It was okay."

"What did you learn?"

"Well, I got acquainted with the classmates through self-introductions. I had to repeat mine several times since I spoke too softly. I was made fun of as a result and have been given a nickname."

"I am sorry to hear this, but I am not surprised. One thing about going to a larger school is you will be interacting with children from different lifestyles and beliefs than your own. You will learn there are different ways to look at a topic. None are wrong in most cases; they are different and perhaps will be foreign. You have repeatedly stated you want to learn more about the world. This is your chance. Be open to others' opinions, but do not let them influence your understanding of yourself too negatively.

"This is an exciting time, and I recommend you treat each day as an experiment. One where you reflect on what happens and digest it as to whether there is a change you desire to make about yourself, or if you wish to remain as you are. I am so proud of you for being willing to experience this school and trust tomorrow will be much better if you approach it as a learning lab, and not as a dreaded place to have to spend time."

Mother is so wise. She knows exactly what to say to make me feel better. I skip on my way to the barn to do the evening chores.

The following school day goes better. Our teachers have us reintroduce ourselves, but this time using only our first names. We break into small groups based on age; my group has five students, including Michael. He says hello to me as the group gathers. I say hello in return. We spend an hour working on arithmetic—one teacher staying with our group while the other works with a group on their spelling skills. From time to time, I glance at Michael to find him looking at me. I avert my eyes, as I do not want him to think of me as being forward. I am glad he seems to want to get to know me though.

Chapter 7
Evening Meal—September 1938

It is customary in our home for the girls to do meal preparation, service, and clean-up. I find this activity to be one of creativity and reflection. I enjoy helping to plan menus for the week—we get needed ingredients from the local store, as well as ensure our garden, when in season, produces desired vegetables and herbs. My sisters and I learn basic cooking skills from Mother. I reflect on the day as I prepare the different dishes, set the table, and clear the table of dishes after supper. Having this quiet time, as well as time with my sisters and Mother, gives us a chance to share what has happened in our lives and to discuss what is happening in others.

Our meals always include meat—beef, pork, or chicken—potatoes, and vegetables. We call lunch *dinner*, and dinner *supper* and soda is *pop*. Everyone works on the farm, helping to plant, till, and harvest crops such as soybeans, hay, and straw, and tend to the livestock. We raise cows, pigs, roosters and hens, and horses. Feral barn cats and pet dogs add to the animal menagerie. Appetites are enormous, and it takes quite a lot of food to satisfy the hunger generated by the hard labor.

Minutes before a meal is served, one of the girls rings a bell hanging in the yard close to the barn. We ring the bell several times, so it is heard. The boys and Father arrive soon thereafter.

Today is no exception. I am the one who rings the bell; we wait for the crew to descend to eat. "Looks mighty good," my oldest brother Aaron states. "I am famished!"

"Let us say grace before this food gets cold," Father says. "June, will you say grace tonight? You and your sisters prepared what appears to be a delicious and substantial meal."

"Glad to Father," I reply. It is an honor to be called upon to offer grace, and I am pleased to be asked to do so. "Let us bow our heads."

> *Our Father, who art in heaven, hallowed be thy name. Bless our family as we gather to partake of tonight's supper. We cherish our communion with one another, as well as with you. Protect those in need, our friends and extended family, and thank you for providing for us. Amen.*

"Could I have more bread and jam," my youngest brother Thomas begs. "I could eat a horse." Our horse Chester whinnies, making us all laugh. "Only kidding Chester – I would never eat you."

"So, how was school today?" Father asks. "What did you learn?"

"Mr. Miller taught us about different types of soil and how to fertilize them depending on what crop one is planting," Aaron replies. "I did not realize there was so much chemistry involved with maintaining ground. Phosphates, nitrogen, acidity—all assist in maintaining good soil. How did you learn about this, Father?"

"Well, my father taught me about this, as I did not attend much school, but instead, helped him with the farm. He had a health condition curtailing what he could do, so I stopped attending school once I finished the eighth grade. I never shared this before as I wanted all of you to get a full education. I regret not having the chance to ask questions and study about the different soil components and their impact on crop growth."

"If there is a particular question you want answered, I will be glad to ask the teacher," one of my other brothers, Jacob, offers. "Mr. Miller knows a lot about soils."

"Thank you, Jacob. I will remember this and appreciate the offer."

"Michael keeps glancing at June during school. I think he likes you, June," Jacob taunts.

"I do not know what you are talking about," I reply blushing.

"Now Jacob, do not tease your sister." Mother quickly diverts the conversation. "Michael was probably looking at her for no reason. Do not go jumping to conclusions embarrassing June."

"Okay, sorry June. I do think he has a sweet spot in his heart for you."

I find myself reflecting on Jacob's comment as I wash the dishes. Does Michael pay more attention to me than the other girls? He is pleasant and seems like a kind person. Subliminally processing the day, I dream Michael visits to ask Father for his blessing for us to be united in marriage.

Chapter 8
Going to Town—April 1943

"I am heading to town today to get grain processed into food for the silo. Any one care to ride along with me," Father asks at breakfast on a Saturday. Since I do not have school, I jump at the opportunity.

"I would be glad to join you, Father. Let me clear the breakfast dishes and get a shawl."

Father can be quite entertaining with his stories of life. While riding into town, he shares one about his youth and how he was sweet on a girl other than Mother. I am at first surprised he could have cared so deeply about someone else, but then realize how naive I am. "What made you like her, Father?"

"Her name was Sadie; she was a cousin of a friend from the meetinghouse. She visited during a conference. I glanced over at her and knew I wanted to get to know her. I was too shy at the time though, so I did not say a word. I told my friend who let Sadie know of my interest. Talk about embarrassing moments. I share this story with you, June, as you are attracting boys due to your beauty and demure nature.

I think it is time for you to have a conversation with Mother about life and recommend she talk with you soon. Okay?"

"Sure Father. I think I understand what you mean, and I really appreciate your kind words about me. This means a lot. I do want to please you and Mother with what I do. I will ask Mother to talk with me."

Mother wants some items from the general store, including sewing thread and fabric, as well as flour, spices, and lard. Father drops me off at the store before he goes to the feed mill. I am to meet him at the mill when I am done shopping, as the grinding of grain and blending of food for the silo takes time.

As I enter the general store, the owner, Mr. Lehman, and his wife greet me with news of what items are on sale, including the type of fabric Mother wants. I have three yards of it cut while I continue shopping. I gather quite an armful of goods. After paying for them, I attempt to lift the wrapped package to head to the mill, when the store door opens, and a young gentleman enters.

"Peter, your appearance is timely," the owner exclaims. "Would you help June with her package? She is going to the feed mill to meet her father but has quite a handful and could use some help."

"Glad to help her," Peter says. "I want a pop. If you can wait for me, June, I'm all yours."

"Why I can carry this myself, thank you. I am not as helpless as Mr. Lehman thinks. I do not want to take you away from your errands."

"Don't be silly. Errands can wait. Here's the pop I want...say, is it still five cents, Mr. Lehman? Now let me take the big package. See ya when I'm in town again, Mr. and Mrs. Lehman!"

I reluctantly hand the package to Peter, who treats it like a feather. He leads the way out of the store and heads towards the feed mill.

"Apparently, you have been to the feed mill before?" I ask.

"I have. I live about a half-hour from here. How is it you're heading to the feed mill on such a beautiful day—almost as beautiful as you are?"

Peter's comment about my beauty embarrasses me and I become silent. When I recover, I say "You are being too kind. I came to town with my father, John Davis. We live about a mile from here. My mother needed some items from the general store. Thank you for helping me carry these items to the feed mill, but you do not need to. I can handle them."

"Don't be serious. I always like helping a fine lady in distress. I'm happy to lend a hand. What all did you buy, may I ask?"

"Oh, some ingredients for baking and some sewing notions and fabric."

"I bet what you sew and cook look as good as you do."

Immediately, I feel the heat in my face as I turn crimson. "I enjoy aiding Mother with the household chores and find cooking to be a creative outlet. Sewing is necessary, but I prefer to cook."

"Maybe I'll get lucky, and someday soon you'll invite me to taste your fine cooking. Give me a holler—you won't have to ask me twice," Peter jokes. "Let me get the door—great talking with you, and I hope to see you again soon."

I enter the feed mill and think to myself, *Yes, I ought to ask Mother about men, and perhaps sooner rather than later.* Peter has awakened a feeling in me I scarcely understand, yet, truth be told, I find myself enjoying it.

Chapter 9
Repentance—May 1943

All I can think about is Peter. How could a chance meeting spark so many emotions within me? My daydreaming has intensified, both in volume and in types of scenarios. I see myself being married to Peter and daydream about what our life would be like. I envision us living in a city, with stores, restaurants, and museums within walking distance. I see beautiful children who attend regular school and take part in sports and musical activities. We enjoy a lifestyle full of fun. I realize such a marriage would not be viewed favorably by my parents, as Peter is not part of the Plain Faith. In fact, I do not know what Peter believes. I have got to stop these fantasies soon.

Peter seems so full of life and vigor and has an energetic spirit I have not witnessed in Plain men. When I compare Peter to Michael, Michael seems so serious and righteous. He would be a good husband and father I am sure, but life would be a continuation of what it currently is—composed of family, farm, chores, and meetings. With Peter, I would be challenged mentally and would experience so many things I have not to date. Or at least I think that is what would happen. I do need to talk with Mother about how one feels when in love as Father suggested, as I am afraid of where I am heading.

"Everyone ready? We are going to be late," Father barks. "I will get the car started, so do not tarry." It is a beautiful spring Sunday, and we are headed to the meetinghouse for services. The meetinghouse was built by men within the community to serve as a place of worship. It is collectively owned and managed, as each family contributes to its operating costs.

"I am ready," I state and head to the car so I can get a good seat. Father beats me to it; he and I are the only ones for a couple of minutes.

Father takes this opportunity to talk with me about Michael. "I expect you will see Michael today at services. I hope you have asked Mother to have a talk; if you have not, this is a reminder to ask her to do so soon. Michael is a fine young man, and one we would welcome into our family if you agree he is of interest to you. He comes from a good Plain family and his father has held religious positions with grace. You need to be thinking about courting for you are getting older."

"Thanks Father. I plan to ask Mother to talk with me. I hear what you are saying about Michael and am glad to know you would be willing for me to date him if there is interest."

Internally, I am conflicted. I am glad to know how Father feels; he so rarely expresses any of his thoughts. Michael would be a good mate for me as far as expectations. But I keep thinking of Peter. One meeting and I am smitten; I feel very confused.

We arrive at the meetinghouse early, so there is time to greet others outside of the building before the services begin. I see two friends—Sally, whose proper name is Sarah, and Beulah.

"Hi, Sally and Beulah," I yell.

Sally replies, "Hey there. Glad you made it. Looks like a lot of people are here already. This weekend has flown. Yesterday, I helped Mother bake and get ready for our Sunday meal. I am anxious to get back to class tomorrow though. I am not sure I did well on the arithmetic test we took last week. Mr. Miller said he will have our grades ready by tomorrow."

"I have been busy too," Beulah contributes. "I baked cinnamon rolls and planted some flowers in the garden. We cannot wait to have fresh herbs and vegetables. Otherwise, just another weekend for me. How about you?"

"I went to the general store with Father. I am also anxious about the arithmetic test. I fear arithmetic is not my best subject. Hope we get our grades tomorrow as promised." I almost share about meeting Peter but quickly retreat; I need to remain silent about him until I learn more, if I ever get the chance to see him again.

Entering the meetinghouse, we hear Michael's father command, "All rise as we recite the Lord's Prayer," as he is the current minister of our meetinghouse. He was chosen through an elaborate selection process from among all the men in attendance. If you are chosen to serve as the minister, it is expected you accept. It is seen as a calling from God to serve. It's a commitment of time, and most men are more than happy to not be selected. Community members come to you for advice and counsel, and assistance on deciding when to seek aid from the bishop. The bishop is a trained individual who interacts with more than one meetinghouse. Michael's father is the current minister, meaning my father would have to go directly to him to bless a marriage between Michael and me. Normally, fathers of the couple would discuss the commitment, agree to it, with the girl's father approaching the minister to seek his approval.

I evaluate Michael's father with new eyes—what would he be like as a father-in-law? As a grandparent of our children? And what about his wife—is she someone I think I could be close to if I did marry Michael? Is she a kind person, one whom I could confide in over the years? If I marry Peter instead, what would Father have to do? Would he still need permission from our minister, and would he be able to get such as Peter is not Plain? I seriously doubt it.

"June, please sit," Mother quietly asks me. I am shaken out of this daydream and realize everyone else is seated. I am embarrassed and soon find myself asking God for forgiveness for even thinking of Peter when I know he would want me to remain in the Faith of our ancestors. I repent and ask God to forgive me and give me strength to see only good attributes in Michael, so I can fall in love with him. I continue to seek forgiveness on the ride home.

As Mother says prayers at bedtime, she mentions me and asks God to help me with whatever is troubling me. She perceives my floundering emotions. I did not realize how obvious I was with today's daydreaming. I make a mental note to ask for time alone with Mother.

Chapter 10
Chance Encounter—October 1943

Once a year, our meetinghouse joins with others in the area to hold a conference. This conference follows a national one that rotates throughout the country. This year the national conference, the 157th one, was held in McPherson, Kansas, from June 7-11. Since local farmers find it difficult to leave their animals and travel during the warm weather, a local annual mini-conference is held in a campground near where we live.

The campground includes several meeting pavilions, a camp kitchen, a dining hall, and several covered areas with picnic tables for eating meals. Numerous cabins can be reserved by those who travel a distance. Since our house is near the campgrounds, our family has never stayed in one of these miniature homes, but I have seen the inside of several, as I visited with friends' families from time to time.

The intent of the conference is to offer an opportunity to renew one's faith and commune with others to explore various worldly topics, as well as religious ones. There is singing, sermons given by ministers and bishops, and hours of Bible study. The young children perform a play on the final night.

They are excited about being "on stage," and it is delightful to see the pride on their parents' faces.

This year, our local discussions will reflect several topics covered at the national conference. These topics relate to the current world war, such as offering support for conscientious objectors involved in Civilian Public Service (CPS), and what role we should play in providing relief to populations impacted by the war. I look forward to attending this conference to learn more about what is happening in Europe.

The local conference is held in October when most of the crops have been harvested and the weather is cooler but not freezing, for the cabins and buildings are rugged. Most cabins are outfitted with two or three double beds, one or two sofas, some comfortable cushioned chairs, and a small dining table with wooden chairs. The only circulating air comes in through screened windows and doors. Some cabins include fireplaces, but not all. Those without fireplaces are outfitted with a woodstove to help heat the cabin at night.

The cabins are clearly meant to be a place to sleep and not much more. Attendees are encouraged to join in the lessons and events, and to engage with other conference attendees, not one's immediate family. Meals are served in a dining hall.

Today's program includes Bible study sessions followed by a communal supper with a high bishop from the Faith's administrative offices.

I wake early in my home and dress before the other family members stir. With a glass of orange juice in my hand, I enjoy the multifaceted colors of the sunrise from the porch. Life on the farm starts with the rooster crowing, the hens guarding their eggs, and the cattle mingling and chomping on the dry meadow grass. My horse is waiting at the gate. I rub his head. "Hi Sparky. How is my boy this morning? Did you get a good night's sleep?" Sparky nuzzles my hand looking for a carrot or sugar lumps. Pulling two lumps from my shawl pocket, I hold them for Sparky to consume; he does so within seconds.

"Feeding the livestock huh? Isn't it early to give him sugar?"

I twirl around, surprised to hear his voice. I see Peter coyly looking at me. "How did you get here and what do you want?" I ask.

"What, I can't drop by to wish you a happy conference? I hear many people are in town to attend the annual conference, and I figured you will be heading there soon. I was hoping to get to see you before you get consumed by the pomp and circumstance. I have been thinking of our meeting at the feed mill back in April, and I wanted to be sure you didn't think I was being assertive by inviting myself to taste your cooking. My gut tells me you are a terrific cook. I know I'm being forward here, but you have been on my mind ever since."

I duck my head; I am speechless. A man has never said this to me, let alone a stranger. I need to conceal how much his words please me. I do not know him or who he is, yet my heart beats faster, and I am thrilled by his attention.

"Yes, we are going to join the conference today. I thought I would wake early to take care of Sparky. I am surprised you are here—how did you get down the lane without anyone hearing you?"

"When a guy is motivated, there is a way. I rode a bike so I would be quiet and not disturb others. It's lying there in the tall grass, getting wet from the heavy dew. I had a feeling you would be awake early; my intuition was correct—here you are. I wanted to see you to be sure you are as lovely as I remember. And you are."

"Well, I suggest you get your bike and go home, for the family will soon depart for conference. I do not want them to see you. You need to leave, and now. I am sorry you came the whole way here to see me, but I cannot speak with you any more. Please go. Please."

"Okay, Madam. I know when I've been dismissed, even if it was done politely. I hope you'll continue to think about me, because I'm going to find ways to see you. You have caught my fancy, and I'm not one to easily surrender. Until we meet again, be safe, and enjoy the show as they say. No harm intended. And don't be surprised if I happen to appear during conference; trust me, I will be discreet. Bye for now."

Peter gets on his bike. I turn around to watch him leave, as I examine and attempt to deal with these foreign feelings. How can this boy get to me with so much unknown about him? Conference will give me time to reflect. I go inside to get dressed for the "show."

Chapter 11
Conference—October 1943

Father parks our car in the temporary parking lot created out of a field. We pile out ready to start the day. There is Miriam, a friend of mine, and her family. I ask if I may sit with her during the opening service. She seems delighted to have my company. Our families join the rest of the conference attendees outside the main meeting pavilion where the bishop from our sect's administrative office is about to speak. He is usually very engaging and encourages us to repent for our past sins and to learn how to avoid future ones.

The crowd gets the signal to enter the pavilion. We do this in an orderly and respectful fashion. While the meeting pavilion is not our normal meeting place, we treat it with the same respect—as a place of worship and a house of God. We find seats—wooden benches lined in rows of 20 deep and four sets across with aisles separating the sets. The pavilion holds around 150 people, roughly three times larger than our regular meetinghouse. The sound carries, even the quietest whispers. Miriam opens the hymn book she brought along to the page announced by the choir leader. The choir sings the first verse of the hymn, and we all join in singing the chorus and the remaining verses *a cappella;* there are no musical instruments to accompany us. The sound resonates against the wooden beams and ceiling of the pavilion, giving me goosebumps. Beautiful music for the Lord.

After more singing, the bishop delivers a moving talk about how we are God's creations, and thus we need to be sure to lead our lives as children of God would—do unto others as you would have them do unto you. He has a directive for different audience members. Children—respect your parents, religious guides, and teachers. Parents—teach your children kindness, charity, and establish within them a deep faith from which they can draw when times are difficult. Communities—help one another to be better as a whole unit than your individual parts. Look out for one another, help one another, share riches such as fruitful harvests when possible, and protect each other from harm. Wives—respect and honor your husbands, and husbands—return these practices to your wives. In our religion, men and women are seen as equal, as far as within the familial unit, but men can hold appointments in the meetinghouse and be employed outside of the home. They are ultimately responsible for their family's activities. Women are to take care of their families and their households first, but they can run small businesses, such as baking goods to sell at the local farmer's market or restaurants showcasing home-cooked meals for tourists. Our sect of the Anabaptists is more liberal in how men and women are treated than the others—the Amish and Mennonites.

When the bishop is finished with his inspirational delivery, we adjourn for a half hour to use the outhouses, chat with each other, and prepare our minds for Bible study. This study is done by age groups—parents, teenagers, pre-teens—with those under six being entertained by volunteer mothers to practice their parts for the final day's event.

Miriam and I head to a bench under a tree when she is greeted by another friend who pulls her aside to talk. I walk toward the bench to get some fresh air before entering the smaller meeting pavilion. The birds, including cardinals, are chirping loudly but beautifully, as if they have been inspired by the bishop's talk. Even the squirrels seem playful and full of energy. I am about to throw an acorn to a squirrel when I hear "Hello there." Startled, I see Peter coming around a maple tree behind the bench.

"Didn't mean to scare you, but I told you I would be visiting you periodically. Guess you didn't think it'd be this morning again. But as I was riding away from the farm, I thought: you can either let June alone or keep telling her how much she's been on your mind. As you can tell, since I am here I decided to keep trying to see you."

"Peter, you cannot be here. This is a conference for Plain people, and you are not Plain. Others may see us; I am not to speak with strange men. Will you please leave now?"

"Brushed off again, huh? Okay, I get it, but when can I see you so we can chat longer in order for you to get to know me? Can we meet in town someday soon? If you can get a ride, I will meet you—name the time and place. As you don't have a telephone to ring me, I'll stop by the farm, like I did this morning, early next week to see if I can get a date set with you. Not a real date of course, but a chat date. No harm, right? Assume this fits your religious beliefs and doesn't cause you to be a sinner," Peter says with a grin. "Last thing I would want is to send you to hell."

Hell—he said *hell*. Flustered, I reply, "Please go now. I will think about what you have asked if you will leave immediately."

"Great, my work here is done. Get some good religion while you're here. I look forward to our future meeting—your place, your druthers. Meanwhile, please know I won't be getting any rest from thinking about you. You have made an impression on my soul."

Within minutes of Peter's departure, sister Rachel comes over to call me to the Bible study session. I gather my dress, but more so, my wits as I try to focus on the lessons to come and not the man occupying my thoughts. Peter, how can you do this to me? You are a stranger, but someone I desperately want to get to know.

Chapter 12
Supper Talk—October 1943

Mother, sisters, and I are buzzing around the warm kitchen preparing a hearty meal for the men, as they are baling hay today. Hay baling is demanding work. Lifting the bales as they are produced and stacking them neatly onto a flat-bed wagon requires arm muscle strength. One person drives the tractor pulling a hay baler, while others load the wagon. Once the wagon is full, the hay is taken to a hay mow to be used for winter storage.

Each side of our barn has a large hay mow. At the beginning of the harvest season, the hay bales are loaded individually onto an open elevator with a conveyor belt. The hay bale is lifted into the air and dropped onto the hay mow floor. Once bales are dropped, they are arranged in stacks to maximize the hay mow storage capacity. The hay must be dry, or it can self-combust into a fire. Barns have been lost to such fires.

As the harvest season continues, the height of the haystacks increases, and the hay bales do not drop far into the now packed hay mows. Lifting a bale above one's head to stack it is arduous work delegated to Father and my brothers. They are ravenous from this exertion.

It is 7 p.m. and dark outside. The entire wagon had to be unloaded as there is intense rain predicted for tomorrow.

"What smells so good?" asks Father. "We are famished and ready for some good home cooking!" "Oh boy, home-made biscuits," exclaims Aaron. "Please pass the gravy so I can bury these biscuits in it."

"Now wait a minute," Mother interjects. "We need to say grace first, and Aaron, since you are so energetic, will you do the honors?"

"Sure Mother, I am glad to do so. Please clasp your hands, bow your heads and join me in thanking the good Lord for the harvest today and the delicious reward awaiting us. *Dear Father in Heaven…*"

The meal is consumed in record time as everyone is famished. As I clear the dishes, Jacob states, "June, did I see you talking to Michael during the one conference break? Do you like him? It seems like you two were talking about something important. I saw you were leaning close to each other. What is the story? Are you and Michael going to court each other?"

"Now Jacob, can you not see you are embarrassing your sister. She has the right to talk with whomever she wishes," Father says in my defense.

"Well, if you ask me, there is something happening between them, and may I be the first to say I think Michael is a fine man and would be a great husband for you, June. He comes from a good family, works and studies hard, and is well liked by the other students and members of our meetinghouse. You have my blessing to date him if you want," Aaron comments.

"Since when are you the head of the household?" Father jokingly asks Aaron. "While I agree with you, Michael is a great citizen and a respectable individual, it is June's decision if she wishes to be pursued by Michael. June, if you want, I can meet with Michael's Father to get permission for a courtship."

"Father, I would like to get to know Michael better, and since I have Aaron's approval, please do go ahead and talk with Michael's father. But let me know when you are going to approach him. Meanwhile, Aaron, let the selection of companions be my responsibility. You do not need to protect me, brother. I am old enough to look out for myself."

I end the conversation before things get too dissected by my other siblings. One of the problems of being a middle child is the advice you get from your older siblings and parents. I know Aaron means well, but I feel Michael is being pushed on me and my thoughts are not with him, but with Peter. However, no one in the family knows about Peter, so I must play along and act like Michael could be my future husband.

Chapter 13

Michael and the Family—November 1943

One of our neighbors invites my family to a harvest supper, as the crops are very abundant this fall. When we arrive, I see Michael and his family are also guests. There are many other neighbors and members of the meetinghouse in attendance. Several tables have been set up in the house with a huge array of food on each one. The meal is a buffet with lots of home-cooked dishes: salads and main dishes, and of course, all kinds of homemade desserts, including pies and cakes. It is a potluck of sorts. Mother brought her famous corn pudding to contribute to the feast.

Not long into the evening, Michael works his way through the crowd and asks if he can sit beside me at supper. What can I say? It would be rude not to invite him to join our family. With everyone watching us closely, it is expected he and I will share time together. While the experience is a little overwhelming, as I have never shared a man with my family as a companion, they seem comfortable around him. My brothers find many things in common with him, and by evening's end, I like Michael. He is easy to talk to and asks me several questions about myself. He is very polite and a true gentleman. Perhaps, I do need to give him a chance.

Chapter 14
Chance Encounter II—November 1943

Waking early is never a problem as our rooster thinks it is his job to announce the sunrise to the world. Rolling over, my last dream comes vividly to mind. Michael and I are holding hands walking down a street laughing at the children playing nearby. He turns to me and says, "I cannot wait until we have our own children. I know you will be a terrific mother, and I want to be the best father to them."

This morning it was the dream that made me wake, not our rooster. It is very unsettling, because I do not have strong feelings toward Michael. He is a nice young man and a kind person, but I am realizing Peter is dominating my heart; it is he who drifts into my frequent daydreams. I see us as parents of a fine brood of children, not Michael and me. What am I going to do? My parents want me to like Michael; he shares our values and our beliefs. Peter is so different and worldly. He makes me smile and intrigues me; his interests are so different from what I know. I want to spend time with him to learn more about him, but it is not possible. My fate is unknown; I need to start the day.

"What do you want for breakfast," Mother inquires. "Your Father and brothers are already off to the livestock market. Your sisters have eaten, and I am afraid there is nothing left of what I had cooked, so what would you like?"

"I will have hot oats with fruit, but I am happy to help myself. Go ahead with your chores, and I will soon get to mine."

Mother smiles and asks, "I might get a ride into town to get some flour and other baking supplies. Would you care to join me?"

"Mother, how fun. Let me grab something to eat, so I do not hold you back. I will have cold cereal and get dressed quickly."

The town is hopping; people are drifting from store to store. Mother enters the general store. I wait for her on the bench on its front porch. The day is not too cold yet and the chickadees in the trees are singing as a chorus. I am thinking about the dilemma with Michael when I hear a muted whistle from around the side of the store. I approach slowly. Who is there, but Peter.

"What are you doing here?" I ask.

"Seeing you, of course. I thought today was a shopping day for your mother, and I was hoping you would be joining her, and we could get to chat a little while she is shopping, so stay where you are, and I'll come closer but will stay hidden."

"You should not. If I get caught talking to you, there could be trouble."

"Let's take our chances. Tell me what you have been doing the last couple of weeks?"

"Just doing chores, helping with the housework, and making a few crafts. And attending meetinghouse events...the usual. How about you?"

"I've been busy myself with work. I'm working with my Uncle Arthur at the feed mill, hoping we might be able to see each other more often. You could come to town with your father when he gets supplies for the farm. I want to learn more about you and talk to you, as you are all I think about. You have become an obsession. Is this possible?"

Blushing, I shyly reply, "I can try. I want to be with you without Father catching us talking. I would like to get to know you also. I cannot be too forward, and even this exceeds my comfort level. I am not one to talk to strangers."

"Who are you calling a stranger? I see I have a lot of work to do. I'm getting the feeling this is going to be complicated, but I want to see more of you and am willing to take the risks, whatever they may be."

"June, can you come inside a minute? I want your opinion," Mother shouts.

I give Peter a farewell signal and go into the store, leaving my heart on the porch.

Chapter 15

Tipping Point—November 1943

Life on a farm is never dull. There are chores needing attention, and when they are done, there is needlework, sewing, or reading. I find I treasure these creative times. They offer a chance to reflect and put things in perspective.

Tonight, I am embroidering a pillowcase. Items like this will become part of a hope chest for use when I am married. The purpose of the needlework causes my mind to wander back to my recent encounter with Peter. My feelings toward him are strengthening. Can it be love? I know it is a different feeling than when I am around Michael. When I am in Peter's presence, my heart skips beats and pumps faster. My hands get sweaty, and my voice rises in pitch. I have never felt this way about any other person before. I wish I understood what this all means.

Peter has seemingly taken an interest in me, at least from what he said. Does he say such words to other girls, though? Is he sincere or is he flirting? How can I make myself have feelings for Michael? It would make things so much easier if I could transfer my interest to him, and not Peter. I want to be married; it is what women do. We provide good homes for our children and our spouse, a home worthy of the Lord. Would being married to a non-Plain person still make this future possible? Is this a future I want or is it one I have been told I want? I cannot believe I am even questioning this, but I am. I am so confused. I must understand these feelings better, get to know Peter more somehow before I divert from any direction planned for me.

I observe non-Plain women in town, and they seem happy with their lives. They seem to be good homemakers and mothers. What will happen to me if I stray from the religion? Will my parents, my siblings, and my friends disown me? Do they not want me to be happy? Is there only one way to please God—to be Plain? Is God so unforgiving of non-Plain individuals? From Bible lessons, I cannot see how God could be judgmental. I know I will lose a lot if I break away from the Faith; but maybe I would gain a lot as well?

Chapter 16
The Talk—November 1943

Mother and I are alone in the house. Everyone else is running errands. I take the opportunity to share the conversation I had with Father back in April and his request she explain relationships between men and women. Mother looks up from her knitting and says, "I knew this time was coming. I was trying to figure out how to talk to you about love and physical attractions. Let us get hot chocolate and sit by the fire. This is a little complicated, and I want to be sure you have a chance to ask me questions."

The hearth is a favorite place for both light-hearted and intense conversations. Here is where I learned about the monthlies and how women use rags to catch the bloody bodily fluid. I recall being appalled I was going to have to experience this every month. Why? This conversation may inform me of the reason for this periodic inconvenience and mess.

"Where should I begin?" Mother says. "The topic we are about to discuss is sensitive, and one a lot of mothers do not do a good job of explaining to their daughters, including mine. To prevent that from happening, I am going to go into a lot of detail. This may be embarrassing to you, but I want to be honest and make sure you know how life truly begins.

"You know about the monthlies and how to prepare for and manage them. We never talked about why you have these periods and their purpose. When adults fall in love, they produce children as you well know. How do these children get created? It is through love and physical connection. A man has a penis, and you have a vagina. When a man gets excited sexually, the penis enlarges and becomes hardened for it to be inserted into a vagina.

"You should only have sex after you are married—once you have reached a point of mutual personal respect and genuine desire. Sex is the insertion of the penis into the vagina with the ultimate release of semen from the man. Semen contains sperm. Sperm are little swimmers who work their way into the vagina to find eggs. If a sperm implants within an egg, it becomes embedded in the uterine wall to produce a fetus. Around nine months later, the female gives birth to a hopefully healthy child. Are you with me? You look a little peaked."

I cannot answer her at first. "Does this mean you and Father had sex to create our family?"

"Yes, sex is a natural part of life, and God's gift to humans to keep generations of families reproducing through the ages.

One Tragic June

Do not be embarrassed about it; instead, cherish and engage in it once you are in love and married."

"So only married women can have babies, am I understanding you correctly?" I do not think this is the case, but from Mother's description, I need to clarify.

"Well, that is the best scenario and one our Faith abides by. However, since sex is a physical experience, as well as an emotional one, women can become pregnant if they have sex. There are some measures to prevent pregnancies, which I will describe when you get closer to the time, but there is always a chance when you have sex. But yes, unwed women can become pregnant."

"But what do the monthlies have to do with becoming pregnant? Do you have to be bleeding to have a child?

"No, the opposite. The monthlies or periods are the body's way of removing unfertilized eggs. It sheds the eggs along with the buildup of bloody tissue within a uterus if a fertilized egg does not become implanted in the buildup."

"Okay, wait. Fertilizing and implanting—sounds like farming. Since you said sex is natural, it's understandable the growing of crops and children share some common vocabularies. But how many sperm fertilize an egg?"

"Only one in most cases. However, multiple births such as twins, triples, and quadruples result when more than one sperm penetrates an egg. Hundreds of sperm are released in the semen ejected from a penis. A man releases the tension in his hardened penis by having an orgasm. This sends the semen and sperm swimming into the receiving vagina and ultimately the uterus."

"Mother, this is so embarrassing but extremely interesting. May I think about this some more and have another chat, as I am sure questions will surface as I ponder these facts. I do appreciate your taking the time to talk about this and your openness."

I am in a daze and think I had better not fall in love with anyone, or I could get pregnant.

Chapter 17
Talk Revisited—November 1943

"June and I had a talk today about sex. She mentioned you had asked her to request such a while back. I am afraid I may have scared her with my frankness. I wanted to instill within her proper reverence for the act. I emphasized she needed to be married and in love prior to committing it. She may look a little different at you, as she seemed appalled we had sex to produce our seven children. Not sure she understood we have had sex for more than producing children."

"Thank you, Rebekah, for talking with her. She seems to be paying more attention to boys, and we do not want her to be carried away emotionally without understanding the repercussions. It was so hard for me to resist having sex with you until we were married. I loved you so much and wanted to express it physically numerous times."

"I know, John. I felt the same way. I am so glad we were guided by our commitment to the Lord and waited until we were married. Heaven knows, we could have had nine plus children."

"Indeed, I do love you so much and thank the heavenly Father for the children he blessed us with, even though they can be a challenge. They keep me working hard to supply a home and food. Do you think June is aware of how strong a physical attraction can be and how one can succumb to one's feelings if not careful?"

"I sure hope so, John. She requested time to think about what we discussed, and we agreed to talk again. I am sure she will have questions. She is an inquisitive type, as we well know."

"Again, thank you for doing this. I guess we wait and see what she comes back with and hopefully, time will be on our side, as she is still not seriously courting anyone."

Chapter 18
The Talk Again—December 1943

"June, I need some more sugar and flour to make cookies for the upcoming farm sale. The meetinghouse is hosting a food stand. If Father drops you at the general store while he goes and gets salt licks, will you get these items, plus butter?"

. "Sure Mother, I would be happy to go to the store. Maybe I can go with Father to the feed mill?" Secretly I am hoping maybe I will run into Peter again.

"Great, I think Father is about ready to leave, so finish dinner and I will see you when you all return. I can bake the cookies later this evening, since the sale is not until this weekend."

As we are riding to town, Father says, "I heard you talked with Mother about the facts of life recently. Do you have any questions for me?"

"Mother did give me a lot to think about. I am still a little confused about how children are created. It's hard for me to talk about it with you. I feel embarrassed."

"It is a natural thing, June. No need to be embarrassed. It is important though, you realize the danger you could find yourself in if a man wants to be near you in body, and you do not want to reciprocate. The good news is those within our Faith all learn the benefit of waiting for marriage, so the chances of you having relations outside of your wishes are slim."

"Wait, you mean someone may try to be close with me without me wanting them to? Mother said this only happens when two people are in love and consent to wanting to be together. I did not know a man could force me to do this."

"I did not mean to alarm you, but this happens and when it does, it is called rape. Two adults need to consent to being joined for it not to be rape. But again, with our strong Faith, I believe any man you will court will share the commitment to wait for marriage."

"I wonder who among my friends know about this." says June.

"I would not ask your friends if I were you. This sharing of knowledge is a private family matter. You would not want to upset the families of your friends. Their parents need to talk to them."

"You are right, Father. I will not talk about this with anyone Thank you for talking to me. It is important for me to be informed and to be aware of what others may try to do to me."

"Look, we have arrived. I will be back in about 20 minutes to get you. Here is some money; have a pop while you wait for me."

Chapter 19
Happenstance—December 1943

"Well, hello June. How are you today? Are you here to buy groceries for the family?" Mr. Lehman asks.

"Yes, Mother is making cookies for a farm sale and needs flour, sugar, and butter. Will you gather these items for me?"

"I could, but let's let Peter do this for you."

With a big grin, Peter enters from the storeroom, "It's my favorite customer. Hi, June. What brings you here today?"

"I did not expect to see you, Peter."

"Disappointed huh? I thought I would be a pleasant sight. What do you need?"

I go closer to the counter and ask, "What are you doing here?"

He whispers, "I was thinking about how I could see you more often, and it dawned on me I could work in this store. I would see you and make some money at the same time. My Uncle Arthur wasn't paying me at the feed mill."

I gather my composure, lean away from the counter, and say aloud, "You are working for Mr. Lehman. When did you start?"

"Mr. Lehman hired me last week, and I began on Monday. He told me the customers are nice, and he is correct so far. You are one of my first ten."

Trying to recover from my surprise, I blurt out, "I need flour, sugar, and butter."

"Planning to bake, are you? What are you making and when should I stop by for a sample? I love eating home-made goodies."

"Mother is making cookies for a neighbor's farm sale on Saturday, I am not. I heard there are going to be a lot of people coming to see the farm equipment to be sold as well as their home furnishings. They are moving into a smaller house in town."

"A farm sale you say, on Saturday. Where exactly is this?"

"It's the Grover farm on Sawmill Road, several farms away from ours. We will miss them dearly but wish them the best in their new home. Having a farm to manage was getting too hard on Mr. Grover. I wonder who we might get as new neighbors."

"You are chatty today. It's nice. Well, here are the three items you requested. What else can I help you with?"

"What time is it?"

"Boring ya, huh? I just got started…"

"Not true. Father said he would return in about 20 minutes when he dropped me off. I think I have time for a pop. He said I could have one if I had to wait. Could I have a birch beer?"

"Happy to get that for you. As luck would have it, it's my break time, so okay if I join you?"

"I guess it is."

Peter opens two pop bottles and sets them on a little table in one corner of the store. I look over at Mr. Lehman, who nods and proceeds to the cash register to cover the store while Peter takes his break.

"Tell me a tidbit about yourself I don't know," Peter says.

"I am not sure what you care to learn, but I have six siblings. You know Father, but I do not think you have met my mother. Her name is Rebekah; she is a kind, religious person. She works hard, is a great cook, does nice needle work, and is family oriented. What else do you want to know?"

"I want to know about you—what makes you happy? What do you enjoy doing?"

"There is not a lot of free time for me. Helping with the garden, the farm work, tending to the animals, and going to school and religious services take many hours each week."

Mr. Lehman shouted, "June, your father is here. He's parked right outside the front door."

Peter leans in and whispers, "I hope to see you Saturday at the farm sale. I want to keep seeing you as often as I can."

I rise, gather the groceries, thank Peter, and say goodbye to Mr. Lehman before leaving for the ride home. The possibility of seeing Peter so soon excites me.

Chapter 20
Farm Sale—December 1943

"What a glorious day for a farm sale," Father says. "The sky is cloud free, and the sun is shining brightly. It is cold, to be sure, but it will not be freezing. Everyone come to breakfast, so we can get Mother to the sale to manage the food stall. People are going to want to eat her delicious cookies. I know I do; I have been smelling the cinnamon in them all night."

"Oh John, you can have a cookie before the sale. In fact, you can be a taste tester. But you cannot say you do not like them to have me leave them at home for you to eat," Mother says. "Children, wake up. We do need to get to the sale soon."

I roll over in bed and see the sun beaming through the dew-frosted window. In the nearby tree, a Carolina wren is singing a melodious tune, contributing to the beauty of the morning. I take a quick sponge bath and put on a blue wool dress. I hope to see Peter today, and I want to look good if he comes to the sale. My black shoes look so basic, but they are what I have to wear. I envision a day when I can go to a big city and buy a pair of fancy shoes, maybe even heels…but as a Plain woman, it stays a dream.

Once I am dressed, I help Mother serve breakfast to the family. We load into the truck—many of us onto the bed—as Father plans on buying farm equipment and will need space to haul it.

The farm sale is bustling when we arrive. There are rows of cars and trucks parked in the fields, and I see where the food stall is on the sun porch. Members of the meetinghouse have already arrived; I can smell the coffee from a distance. Children are playing in the fields and dogs are frolicking with one another. I ask Mother if she and the other meetinghouse women need any help with the food stall. She declines but asks me to stop by often, as the crowd might become too much for the women to handle. I promise I will, and I begin to examine the items for sale. I hear my friend Sally calling me. I turn to see her standing under a large weeping willow tree.

"Hi Sally. When did you arrive?"

"About a half hour ago. Mother wanted to be sure to get the coffee going early. I am amazed at the crowd. It's supposed to be the sale of the year. This family has lived here for 50 years and over this time, they have accumulated so much. Father said the sale will take at least eight hours, if not longer. Have you seen anyone else from school yet?"

"Not yet, as we just arrived. It took everyone a while to get ready this morning."

"Yes, I know. I was not the most alert person myself. I need to go and check on an item for Mother, but I hope to see more of you as the day progresses," Sally says.

I am left standing under the tree when I hear a different birdcall and wonder, what type of bird makes such a sound? I hear it again and then it dawns on me, it is not a bird at all...it is Peter. I turn around to face him as he comes into view from behind a wagon shed.

"Thought you heard a new bird, didn't ya? It's a new signal to get your attention. I told you I would see you today. I have been looking forward to this meeting. Can you walk with me a little?"

"Well, I should not as people will see us."

"Okay, how are you? How long will you be around today?"

"I am quite good. I just saw a friend. I think I am here for the duration of the sale, or at least until Father decides to buy equipment and haul it home."

"Good. Let's sit by the shed here for a minute. Please tell me more about yourself. What makes you happy? Do you enjoy coming to events like this or do you prefer being in quieter settings? I want to get to know you, and yet I know our chances for meeting are limited."

I am sure I am blushing. "Why all this interest in me? Surely, you are someone who knows a lot of people. I am not that special. I will tell you about me if you tell me about you."

"Fair enough. I'll start, since I see I may be a bit too forward for your taste. I am from Decatur, Georgia. I have a brother and a sister. My parents are also from Georgia originally. Father is a butcher, and Mother keeps the books for his shop. They have a small farm to keep the animals prior to butchering. I'm the first born, and some say the most talkative of the family. I work hard to get what I want. I have never gotten along well with Father, so when I was old enough to help him in the shop full-time, he decided to send me here instead to work with his brother at the feed mill. He thought I might take instructions from my Uncle Arthur better than I did from him. Now it's your turn."

"Interesting. It must be nice to only have two siblings. As I mentioned earlier, I have six and we are constantly having to share things and work to keep the farm running. I dream of a different life where I am free to do as I wish. To be honest, I would like to explore city life. It seems so glamorous to me.

Being able to walk to many stores and eat out at restaurants when and where you want seems like a true luxury."

"You want to spread your wings and explore, huh? I didn't see that coming. I now see a little different side of you. Someone who has adventure within and is a potential scout! I like seeing this aspect of you."

Flustered, I meet his eyes to see if he is serious. My breathing becomes labored, as I see a soul within his eyes drawing me to him as well. "I must go and see if Mother needs me at the food stall."

"Do you have to leave me? We're getting to know each other."

"Yes, I must go. I enjoyed talking with you, but I promised Mother I would check in periodically. Maybe we will see each other later today." I left Peter stymied, as he had a questioning look on his face. I feel bad as I do want to get to know him, but I am so shy and afraid of where this may be heading. I have never felt this way before, and I am mystified how to conduct myself. I do not want to appear to be too forward, and I do not want others to see us chatting for fear rumors will spread among the meetinghouse congregation. Also, Michael may be in the area. I want to avoid getting a bad reputation. Honor is extremely important to my family.

Chapter 21

Arrival in New York City—June 3, 1944

The train to New York City slows down. A conductor walks through the car and announces our arrival will be in 10 minutes. We are to gather our belongings and get ready to disembark. All these unfamiliar terms. Disembark—sounds like what our dog would do when choking.

The gentleman sitting in the seat beside me asks if the duffel bag on the rack above us is mine. I nod it is. He pulls it down and hands it to me. I thank him shyly.

People seem to be moving to the car doors. I do the same. Once I disembark, I glance around for a person looking for me. Father said there would be a man to drive me to the hotel. I see a person standing with a sign stating my last name in the distance. I move toward the person who seems to be approaching me at the same time.

"Miss Davis, I presume?"

"Yes, hello. Thank you for meeting me."

"My pleasure. I'm Sam Burns. I'm glad to drive you to the hotel, the Roosevelt Hotel, located at 45 E 45th Street. It's a wonderful place to stay. I'm sure you will find it to your liking, as it is right in the heart of Manhattan. It was built about twenty years ago and has gotten many complimentary reviews."

I look at him oddly, as I do not know what he means by downtown Manhattan. I thought I was going to New York City. "Is the Roosevelt Hotel not in New York City?"

Laughingly Mr. Burns replies, "Of course, Manhattan is New York City. It's the name for one part of the city. I will be sure to take you to your hotel."

"Thank you," I demurely state. "I am not used to city life, so please forgive me."

"It's quite all right. I will be sure you are safe and will even point out sights along the way. Follow me to the car."

We walk along the outside of the train station for what seems like forever to a parking lot. I see an elegant black car ahead. Mr. Burns dumps my duffel bag in the trunk and opens the back seat door. I am glad I will not have to look at him during the ride. I take a moment to look around and see a mob of people walking along the streets lined with many stores and restaurants. I cannot believe I am in a city. I wish I was here for fun like a vacation. I dread what is going to happen to me, but for now, I refuse to think about it and decide to enjoy the scenery.

"If you look straight ahead, you can see the Empire State Building. It was finished in 1931 and houses offices for numerous organizations. There's a fantastic view of the city offered by using telescopes for a small amount of change. To the right is Times Square where they drop the lighted ball on New Year's Eve. You're close to Broadway, where playhouses offer theater of all kinds. You are in the middle of the activity of New York City. You can't go wrong."

"It is all so overwhelming, but exciting. Thank you for this information."

"Young lady, you're welcome. Look, here we are already at the hotel. I'll pull in front and a bellman will come to get your bag. You can check in at the registration desk. They will issue you a room and take your bag to the room."

"I can carry it; it is not heavy."

"As you wish, but when in Rome, do what the Romans do."

Confused, I say, "But I am not in Rome."

"True. It's a saying we use meaning when you're in a new area, do what the locals do and enjoy."

"I am so sorry. I did not know. Here is money for the ride."

"Wow, you are a trusting person. The ride is only $1.00; here's $4.00 back. Have a wonderful time and thank you for the business."

"Thank you. I appreciate the ride," knowing I will not have a fun time, but the sentiment was nice.

"Welcome to the Roosevelt Hotel. What brings you to the city madam," says the clerk at the registration desk.

"I am here to do some business." This is what Mother told me to tell people if they ask why I am in New York City.

"Great; we do business well in this city. Do you have a room reservation?"

"Yes. I have a room booked under the name of Davis."

"June Davis?"

"Yes."

"I have a nice room for you with a view of the St. Patrick's Cathedral. It is on the 14th floor. Work for you?"

"Do I have to walk up 14 flights of stairs?"

"No, see the elevators over there?"

"I have never ridden one. May I get a lower floor?"

"Okay, I do have a room on the third floor. Will that work?"

"Great, then I can take the stairs."

"Well, you can, but I recommend trying the elevator and going to the top so you can see the view. It is spectacular."

"Oh, okay. I will see if I can do that later. Do I pay you now?"

"No need to pay ahead. It will be $5.80 a night. I see you are staying for three nights, correct?"

"Yes, I may need to stay longer; I do not know for sure at this point. For now, three nights is right."

"Please sign this form and here's your room key. It is room 314. The stairs are on the right, but I can call the elevator for you. Let us know if we can help in any way, as we are here to be of service. Do you want assistance with your bag?"

"No, I can carry it. Thank you and is there a place to eat?"

"A place to eat? The city has a ton of places to eat. But yes, there is a restaurant right here in the hotel."

"Thank you again." I grab my bag and the key, and head to the stairway, looking around the luxurious lobby. This is a beautiful hotel. I see the restaurant sign. I will eat here until I feel a little more comfortable.

When I get to the third floor, I look for room number 314. It is to the right. I open the door and am amazed at how beautifully the room is decorated. It has a double bed, a sofa, and a marble bathroom. I place my bag on the bed and unpack its meager belongings. I hang two dresses and place the other items in the dresser. I feel grimy from the trip, so I shower. The toiletries are amazing; there is a cute bar of soap, shampoo, and body lotion. The flow of the water from the showerhead is double the force of the one at home. If this is city living, I am already in love.

I dry myself with the most luxurious towels I have ever used and put on one of my dresses. I look in the full-length mirror hanging on the back of the bathroom door. Such vanity items are absent in our house. I look good. I quickly chastise myself for even thinking about how I appear. I wish Peter could see me though.

The view from the window includes tall buildings and streets. There are clumps of people scattered on the sidewalks. They seem to be rushing to go somewhere. How different this view is from the one at home. Trees exist but they are smaller than what I am used to and are carefully arranged along the edge of the street to give green color to the miles of plain gray concrete. Starving, I make my way to the hotel restaurant.

Chapter 22
Father Meets Peter—January 1944
Reading, Pennsylvania

Father comes in from the barn shaking the snow from his boots. "Appears I need to get some silage from the feed mill. I will be back in about an hour," Father says.

"Have a good trip," Mother replies. "And if you do not mind, would you stop by the general store and get oats and cornmeal?"

"Yes, of course."

"Hello, John. How are you doing today?" asks Mr. Lehman, the general store owner.

"Doing great. No complaints in the world. My wife tells me we are running low on oats and cornmeal though. Would you get me a pound of each?"

"Happy to, but let me introduce my new assistant, Peter Brandt. Peter, this is Mr. Davis. He's one of our best customers. Please help him get a pound of oats and cornmeal for his lovely family."

"Pleased to make your acquaintance Mr. Davis. I have already met a member of your family at this store, June. In fact, she was one of the first ten customers I helped. She seems like a fine young lady. You're a lucky man to have such a nice daughter."

"How kind of you to say so. I feel lucky indeed. Where are you from Peter?"

"I live close to here now. My Father is a butcher. He owns a small shop in Decatur, Georgia, where I'm from. I moved here less than a year ago to help my Uncle Arthur with his feed mill and now I work here."

"Welcome to the area. I thought I recognized you from the feed mill. I hope you find the area satisfactory. I bet your parents miss you."

"Well, I'm the oldest of three children. Honestly, I think my parents, Ralph and Bertha, were happy for me to go away to give them some more space in the house. I have a brother and sister still at home. They help with the shop while attending school."

"Children are an immense help, for sure. I appreciate mine assisting with farm chores and housework."

"I'm sure you do. June seemed like she would be helpful. How long have you lived here Mr. Davis?"

"Ever since I was a baby. My ancestors helped to settle the land in this area. We have an extended history with the area."

"Do you like farming, and if so, what do you like the most?"

"Great questions. I only know farming. It is what my ancestors have done for generations. In fact, the farm I own was inherited. I would not know what else to do. As far as what is a favorite...there are a couple of things. I like helping things grow. God gave us this great earth. Growing crops and harvesting fruits and vegetables, as well as other plants, makes me feel I am helping God to feed the earth. He gave me the opportunity to produce edible items, and I am more than happy to share the bounty with others. The second thing I enjoy is the animals. Yes, they can be a pain as they break through fences and get loose, or they wake you with their crowing, but they all have personalities and provide so much entertainment. I enjoy watching them grow. It is a rewarding life, although my body reminds me of how hard it can be."

"Farming is certainly not for the weak. Listen, you didn't come here to chat with me all day. Let's get your items and get you on the road."

"Rebekah, I am home and back with your groceries," John says.

"Thank you for getting these few items. How was Mr. Lehman?"

"He introduced me to his new assistant, Peter, who seems like a nice young man and a friendly person. He mentioned meeting June when he first started working. He seems a little keen on her if intuition is correct. Did she mention meeting him?"

"No, no mention at all. You might be reading into things. Besides, he's not of the Faith, so there is no way June could court or be interested in him."

"You are right. Being an overprotective father, I reckon."

Chapter 23
The Revelation—January 1944

"June, please finish the dishes and join me by the fire. I would like to talk to you." Mother says.

"Will do. I should be done in a couple of minutes." What now, I wondered; what have I done? Did a sibling see Peter talking to me at the sale and is squealing on me? Am I in trouble for not reading enough of the Bible last week? I fell asleep finishing the lesson for Sunday, as the day drained my ability to concentrate.

When I approach the hearth, Mother is already there with two mugs of hot chocolate. Oh no, I must be in serious trouble. "What is it, Mother?"

"Relax. I want to have a follow-up chat to our previous talk. Do you have any questions for me?"

"Yes, I have several questions. I do not know quite how to ask this, but how does one know when one is in love?"

"You have been thinking about our talk. Remember, everyone is different. How you feel in love may be different from your friends, and from what I felt. Love can happen at multiple levels. One can feel a special reaction to a person if you are attracted to them physically. This is often termed infatuation. One can appreciate an individual for how they treat you and others."

"How did you know Father was the one for you?" I ask.

"I wanted a man I could trust, someone who would be a good father and friend, and a good provider. He needed to have faith and be Plain. Most importantly, he should care about me and my welfare. He should make me feel special. I courted several men, but none compared to your father. He always had a smile and would ask me how I was doing and how life was treating me. He seemed to want to get to know me, and I realized over time, he was the one for me. I was lucky of course to find such a man, as he has been considerate and trustworthy throughout all we have experienced together. He gave me lovely children, like you, through having sex, of course."

"How do you know, though?" I inquired. "How long did you court and were you scared to get married? Were you scared to have sex?"

"Father and I courted for about a year and a half. From meetings and school, he was the one who attracted me the most. His smile, his demeanor, his work ethic, and the way he treated me all made me fall in love with him; I wanted to marry him. The wedding night is always a little scary, but a good man will try not to hurt you. There can be pain when he first enters you. This initial pain diminishes, and sex can be quite joyful. You feel so close and there is a physical release when you reach orgasm. Men and women can both have orgasms; male ones are more obvious as the penis softens after the sperm are ejaculated. Women can vary on how often they have orgasms and what causes them to do so."

"Thanks, Mother, for being so open about this. May I be as open in return?"

"Of course. What is on your mind?"

"You know Michael, right? He is a member of our meetinghouse."

"Indeed, I know Michael. Do you like him? He would make a wonderful husband."

"I agree. I think he would, but I am not attracted to him. I do not have any special feelings when I am around him. I do not think I could love him. On the other hand, I met someone who makes my heart flutter and makes me smile upon sight."

"Is this someone a member of our Faith? Where did you meet him and what is his name?"

"His name is Peter, and I met him first at the feed mill when I went with Father about a year ago. He works at Mr. Lehman's general store now. I met him again there and at the recent farm sale. Unfortunately, he is not Plain. But Mother, I want to court him. May I?"

"This is quite the news, June. You know I cannot approve a courtship with a man not of our Faith. I am sorry, but please try to forget him and move on. Maybe Michael is not your future husband, but I am sure there are other men for you to meet."

"But Mother, I am swept away by Peter. He wants to get to know me. No one else has ever shown so much interest. What if he is meant for me? I have heard you cannot defy your heart; it feels what it feels. He makes me feel special. What do I do with these emotions, Mother?"

"Pray about it, June. It is important to stay in the Faith. As you know, if you marry out of it, you will be shunned by friends and family. It is not good news I share, but the truth. Pray, and we will keep talking, okay?"

"Mother, you are always the wise one. Thank you. I will pray and ask the Lord for guidance."

Chapter 24
Mother Tells All—January 1944

"John, we need to talk."

"Rebekah, what is happening?"

"I had another chat with June tonight to see if she had any questions about our talk. Turns out she had quite a few. Nothing unexpected. However, she did surprise me with news about thinking she may be attracted to a man."

"Great. I like Michael and am glad she agrees."

"Well, it is not Michael."

"Wait, who is it then?"

"Sit. You were correct. She is attracted to Peter, the new general store clerk."

"But Peter is not of the Faith. This is terrible, a father's worst nightmare! I will forbid her from seeing him anymore."

"John, do not overreact, please. June is our daughter, and while we may not agree with her choices, she is coming of age and needs to explore the world for herself. We have given her a firm religious foundation, but she was born into our Faith and should have the right to choose her own."

"But if she marries a non-Plain man, she will be shunned by her friends and family. Does she realize what she could lose by making this choice?"

"I think she does…but let us not blow this out of proportion. They have not even dated. I think they chatted at the stores and the farm sale. For Pete's sake, she is not marrying him yet. Oops, I did not mean to be funny. I will chat with her more about her thoughts. If she continues to show interest in Peter, we can talk with her firmly about the results of her choice. I have been blessed to know what true love is through my love for you, and if she indeed feels the same way about Peter, in time, I do not want to hurt her by forbidding her to see him. June has a good head on her shoulders. We need to trust she will do the right thing; we can provide her with guidance to ensure she knows the consequences of her decisions, as we have done so far in her life."

"Rebekah, you have always been wise, one of the things I love about you. While I do not like this and am not in favor of her seeing Peter, I will not forbid her at this time from doing so. However, if it gets more serious, I cannot promise how I will respond. I am responsible for this family, and I know the bishop would not approve of a marriage outside of the Faith.

For now, though, we will watch the situation as you suggest, and act when warranted."

"Thank you, John. I believe this is the best way to manage this for now."

Chapter 25
A Taste of the City—June 3, 1944
New York City

My intention was to eat in the hotel, but while I see the restaurant to one side of the lobby, I also notice the front doors. Couples are laughing and businessmen are grimacing as they rush inside to the elevators. They seem like normal, reasonable people. Maybe this is the chance to see a city I have always dreamed about. When else will I have this opportunity? Maybe experiencing city living will squelch any yearning to leave the country. It is still light outside and there are plenty of people milling about. Perhaps I should find somewhere nearby to eat instead of the hotel restaurant.

"May I assist you?" a hotel employee asks. "I am the hotel concierge. I can recommend and make reservations for you at a restaurant or a museum or whatever your heart fancies."

"I do not want to trouble you."

"No trouble at all."

"Do I need to pay you for this?"

"Absolutely not. It is part of the benefit of staying at this glorious hotel. You are smack in the middle of Manhattan, and it would be a shame not to see some of the city sights."

"Well, I am hungry and would like to eat. I do not want to spend much money though, and I want to stay close to the hotel. Is there someplace nearby you would recommend?"

"What kind of food do you desire?"

No one has ever asked me this question. And I am not sure I understand the question. I hesitate to answer.

"Nearby there is a Mexican restaurant, an Italian one, a French one, a German one, and believe it or not, a couple of American ones. Do you want a meal, a sandwich, or a snack?"

"Um, I am unsure. I have not tried any of these foods before." The concierge looks at my dress and Plain clothing, at once assessing I am not very worldly.

"Is this your first time visiting the city?"

"Yes, in fact, any city."

"I see. Let me explain the different ethnic foods. If you like tomatoes, Italian food uses a lot of them and oodles of pasta. French food has rich sauces covering its meat and vegetables. German food includes vegetables like cabbage, potatoes, and red beets. They also like meat. Mexican food includes vegetables and can be spicy, as they use peppers of various varieties. I'm assuming you know American food. Do any of these seem like a possibility?"

To me, German food sounds like what I eat at home all the time. I ponder spices; not sure I want to try them. "I want Italian if there is a restaurant not too far from here."

"Italian it is. You are in luck! There are a couple of restaurants nearby. I will refer you to my favorite. It is called Gusto's and is next door. Exit the front door and make a right. You will see the sign for Gusto's. I will call and let them know you are coming. Your name is?"

"June...June Davis."

"Are you related to Bette Davis? Just kidding..."

I look at her with confusion and ask, "Who is Bette Davis?"

"June, you do need to explore and spread your wings. Bette is an actress who used to perform on Broadway before she moved to Hollywood."

"Sorry, I never heard of her."

"It's okay. I'm calling Gusto's now. They will be expecting you soon."

"Thank you so much. May I ask a favor of you?"

"Of course."

"I admit, I am quite scared of the city. Would it be okay if I let you know when I return? I want someone to be aware of where I am."

"Well, sure. Check in with me when you return. I think you will be safe though; I wouldn't recommend you try Gusto's otherwise. People on the street can help you if you get lost or need help of any kind. New York City is friendlier than people think."

"Thank you so much." She was indeed an example of friendliness. As I exit the front doors, a gentle breeze welcomes me. Birds are singing, and I realize the city has natural things within it just like my home in the country. I see a robin flying from one tree limb to another, and it dawns on me…I am also free for the first time.

Chapter 26
Permission Granted—January 1944
Reading, Pennsylvania

The family gathers around the table for supper. "Do you have a hollow stomach, Jacob?" Father asks. "That is your third helping of potatoes."

"Father, you know I am a growing man. I worked hard this morning in the fields and indeed generated an intense appetite. Would you pass me the meatloaf?" Jacob asks.

"Guess you did earn your keep this morning. Someone is pulling into the driveway. It is Mr. Wenger's truck. I will go see what he wants. The rest of you finish eating," Father says.

I cannot quite tell what is happening, as Mr. Wenger is not a usual visitor or a close friend of Father's, although he is a member and minister of our meetinghouse, so I am curious and anxious at the same time.

I help to clear the table and wash the dishes with my sister, Mary.

"June, what do you think is happening?" says Mary.

"I am not sure. I hope everything is okay with his family. Maybe he is constructing a shed and wants help. I guess we will know soon." Internally, I am getting worried this might have to do with Michael, Mr. Wenger's son. Michael seems to be friendly to me at school, and he hangs around me more.

After ten minutes, Father comes back into the kitchen.

"Father, what did Mr. Wenger want?" I ask.

"June, I need to talk with Mother before we will be able to talk about his request."

My musings go wild. I bet Michael wants to court me, and Mr. Wenger is asking for Father's blessing before we begin. What am I going to do? I feel so trapped. Michael's a nice person, but I do not have any feelings for him. This was confirmed when I talked with Mother about love.

"John, what is it?" asks Mother.

"Rebekah, would you help me in the shed? I will tell you there."

Can a heart beat as fast as mine is and not explode? This cannot be a good sign. Why all the secrecy? Our parents have always been extremely open with us.

"John, you are scaring me. Is everyone okay in the Wenger household?"

"Yes, everyone's health is fine. Joseph asked for my blessing for his son Michael to court June. Apparently, Michael has expressed interest in our daughter. I thought maybe this was coming from the way he glances at June at the meetinghouse. This may be a blessing to us to have her get interested in him versus Peter. What do you think?"

"This is indeed interesting. I think we need to talk to June and see how she feels. If she is open at all to it, it may be a way for her to see if she can love a man from the Faith. Please call her to the shed as I do not want the other children to overhear our conversation."

"June, will you come join us?" Father yells from the shed.

I must comply; I have no choice. I walk towards the shed like I am going to my funeral, feeling total dread.

"What do you want, Father?"

"As you probably guessed, Mr. Wenger came to ask me to give him my blessing for Michael to court you. Should I say yes? He has already discussed this with the bishop, who has given his approval. Michael seems like a nice young man from my perspective."

I look at him and at Mother, who is looking at me strangely. I wonder if she has told Father about my thoughts about Peter. I am trapped, ready to flee; but the imaginary chains around my legs restrain me.

"I do not know what to say, Father. Michael has always been kind to me. I do not know if I am interested in courting him, but I guess I could go out on a few dates to see if I could become attracted to him. I will date him if you and Mother think it is the best thing for me to do."

"I think it cannot hurt, June. You have not dated anyone, and Michael is Plain. If you could grow to love him, it would be good for you and our family. I am glad to hear you are willing to try. I will let Mr. Wenger know. I need to run into town tomorrow for a few things and their farm is nearby."

"Could I go with you? It seems like I should be present to hear what is further discussed."

Father seeks Mother's approval. She nods and says, "Sure."

Chapter 27
Reality Sets In—January 1944

The conversation about Michael makes me want to scream. Instead, I run upstairs and slam the bedroom door. Tears rapidly flow; I cannot breathe. My heart races and my stomach cramps. Reality sets in; I am going to have to court Michael. He is a nice person, but I want to be with Peter. Michael does nothing for me. But I know if I do not court him, my parents will try and find someone else for me. I am old enough to court; it is expected I will marry within a year or two and start a family. The feelings I have for Peter need to be extinguished as I try to show interest in Michael. Lord, why is this happening to me? Why did you bring Peter into my life? Why am I forced to court someone other than who I want to?

Mother raps on the door. "May I come in?"

Wiping my eyes with a hankie, I cough and clear my throat, "Yes, you may."

"June, I know you are upset. I see you are crying. You feel for Peter and yet, you need to recognize all you would lose if you court him instead of Michael. You are aware our Faith does not permit you to court an outsider. The bishop will excommunicate you from the meetinghouse, and your friends will need to stay away from you. We, as a family, will have to disown you and lose all contact with you. Is it worth it to seek Peter's company with this in mind?"

"I am aware of the consequences and agreed to let Michael court me. I am so conflicted though Mother, as I think I am falling in love with Peter. I think about him all the time. When I see him, I get a fuzzy feeling and become giddy. How do I turn off these intense feelings for him and redirect them to Michael? I feel like a hypocrite."

"What you are feeling may be infatuation and not love. You barely know Peter. Perhaps you need to think of Michael when Peter comes to mind. Replace Peter's face with Michael's. List the positive attributes Michael has to offer. I wish I could say run to Peter and enjoy your attraction, but I cannot as he is not of the Faith."

"Love should not be this hard. I hear what you are telling me, as much as I do not want to. I promised you and Father I would court Michael, and I will honor that, but know this is going to be hard."

"You are a strong and disciplined person. Give Michael a chance. You might be pleasantly surprised."

When Rebekah gets back to the kitchen, John asks, "How is June doing?"

"About how you would expect. She is quite upset she cannot see Peter. She has an emotional attachment to him and is struggling to reconcile her feelings. There is no real interest in Michael to date, but she is willing to court him, as she promised, to see if she can grow to like him. The consequence of marrying a non-Plain man is evident to her. She is a smart girl and we need to be gentle with her as she goes ahead with being courted."

"Indeed, we have raised a good child. It is hard for me to understand she is old enough to marry. What happened to our baby?"

"She is maturing. We need to give her room to grow."

"I will try, but she cannot marry out of the Faith. We might lose our standing in the meetinghouse if she does, and we will lose her as a result."

"I am fully aware; I am sorry we are having to force her to court Michael though. We need to handle this situation gently with June, or we will lose her for good."

Chapter 28
Fine Dining—June 3, 1944
New York City

New York City is full of restaurants. Finding Gusto's was no problem. The concierge's directions were perfect. Upon entering the restaurant, the hostess greets me and asks if I have a reservation. I answer one was made for me under the name of Davis.

"I see it right here. Do you prefer a booth or a table?"

"A booth."

"Follow me." I am taken to the back of the restaurant near the kitchen door. There are many diners in all modes of dress. I am the only Plain dressed woman, of course.

"Is this booth okay with you?"

"Yes, this is fine."

"Your waiter should be with you soon. His name is Alberto. Here's a menu meanwhile."

"Thank you."

Alberto appears within seconds, bringing me a glass of water. "Well, hello young lady. Are you expecting others to join you?"

"No, I am alone."

"No problem. In addition to our menu, here is a sheet with our house specials. Have you dined with us before?"

"This is the first time." *And probably the last time I think to myself.*

"This is the place for the best Italian food in the city if I say so myself. I have worked here for over 20 years and have never served a disappointed diner."

"Good to hear."

"Take a minute to review the menu and specials, and I'll be back with some bread and butter to see if you have any questions."

The choices are extensive. I am intrigued with the Italian words for the dishes. To date, I have only had spaghetti. There are soups, salads, appetizers (appears these are smaller plates), entrées, desserts, and drinks of all kinds listed. Where to begin. I cannot spend more money than what Father has given me.

"Does an item whet your appetite?"

"I will have the lasagna with the side salad."

"Great choices. They make the pasta in-house. What type of dressing do you want on the salad? What would you like to drink?"

"Do you have vinegar and oil? And water is fine."

"We do. Enjoy the bread and I'll be back with your lasagna."

The meal is delicious. I have never tasted food like this. The tomato sauce is different than what we cook at home. The spices are blended well. I cannot tell what they are except for pepper. The salad is fresh and the bread warm. Alberto brings me a plate of fresh sliced tomatoes on the house for an appetizer. My dessert is delicious fresh strawberries covered with whipped cream. I pay the bill and leave a tip on the table. As I leave, Alberto tells me to have a good evening and thanks me for coming to Gusto's.

When I get back to the hotel, I let the concierge know I have returned. She asks if I had an enjoyable time. I thank her for the wonderful recommendation and head to the elevator with a bounce in my step. Feeling brave, I decide to take the elevator to my room. The bank of buttons inside the elevator is confusing, but I see a 3 and assume it stands for the third floor.

The elevator starts with a jolt but soon moves; I arrive on my floor in no time.

Tonight, I ate my first solo meal, ordered a new type of food, paid for it, used an elevator, and was treated like a princess. Yes, city life suits me so far, but back to the farm.

Chapter 29
First Date—January 1944
Reading, Pennsylvania

Courting as a Plain woman follows a set of rules and parameters. Michael must come to my home and tell Father where he is taking me and what time we will return. He will describe what we will be doing and who else will be present— just key individuals. Once the date details are shared, Father can adjust or stop the date if he feels it is too risky for me. He has the ultimate say, and Michael must obey my Father's wishes if he wants to continue courting me. This is an accepted sect practice; any other behavior would be questioned.

"Come on in, Michael. It is a pleasure to see you as always," Father says as he opens the door. "How are you doing?"

"Fine, Mr. Davis. Thank you for letting me court June. I feel honored to be able to do so."

"Please take good care of her. We cherish her and trust you will do the same. Where do you two plan to go?"

"I thought we would drive to the band concert in the town hall. There should be a good crowd and different kinds of food booths."

"Sounds like a nice outing on such a beautiful day. Let me call June."

"June, Michael is here."

The moment of dread has arrived. I pull on my dress and shoes and fix pieces of fallen hair from my bun. "I will be down soon." I am delaying as I really do not want to see him.

"Hello Michael."

"Hi June. You look nice. I was telling your father what I thought we will do. Would you want to hear the town band? We can grab food while we listen to them play."

"Sounds like a nice afternoon."

"What time do you expect to return?" asks Father.

"It is 11 now. Would 4 o'clock be okay with you?"

"Sounds fine. Enjoy the day and see you around 4."

Michael politely opens the truck door and offers his hand to help me get into the seat. Touching his hand repulses me. He closes the door and gets into the driver's seat. He smiles at me sheepishly.

"It is about a three-mile drive to the town hall. We will arrive in time to have dinner before we listen to the band. Sound good to you?"

"Yes, I think all sounds fine." I cannot think of what to say. Michael starts the engine, as my parents wave goodbye from the porch. I look at them and try to smile as I wave back; the smile is forced.

"I guess this is a little awkward for you. I know this is our first time courting. I am nervous to be honest. I have not courted much. Let me tell you more about myself."

"Please do."

"You know my family from the meetinghouse, so I do not need to introduce them. Besides helping with the farm, I am working at a local bank a couple of days a week."

"What do you do at the bank?"

"I am a teller, but I hope to become a loan officer. When I interviewed, the manager indicated this might be a possibility. I get to meet a lot of people and like it so far."

"What a great way to learn more about finances, and you have goals for the future. How do you do all of this and farm?"

"Father is flexible with me. He said if I get the chores done, he does not care when I do them. I traded the time-dependent chores, for example, milking, with my brothers. As a result, I clean out stalls, fill feeding bins with hay and silage, and brush the horses among other things. All of this is worth being able to work to make some money to save for a family and a house."

"It is great you are thinking of the future. What do you get to do at the bank?"

"As a teller, I help people with their banking transactions—deposits and withdrawals. I briefly explain the different types of banking accounts, referring customers to the manager for further details if they are interested. My favorite thing is when the young children come in with their piggy banks and dump their savings on the counter. They love to count the change and deposit it. I mark the amount in their savings account book and give them a lollypop in exchange."

"Sounds like you like children."

"I do. I hope to have several of my own someday."

This conversation is headed to a place I want to avoid, so I quickly change topics. "How did you get the teller job?"

"Father talked with the bank president who asked me to interview for the position. The bank manager asked me questions about my arithmetic abilities, values, and goals. I guess I passed his test. I was offered the job within the week. I have worked there for about six months."

"Good for you. I cannot work outside of the home as you know except to help with cleaning houses, or being a cook, or other women-related work. So far, I have helped Mother with managing the home. With six siblings, there is constant cooking and cleaning. I also sew and like to do needlework, especially knitting."

"What do you like to knit?"

"Mostly things we wear like sweaters, shawls, scarves, and mittens. Sometimes I get to do a special piece with good yarn."

"It is good to be able to make and repair clothes." I do not offer a reply.

We ride in silence until the town hall appears. We arrive a little early. The afternoon is pleasant for January, and the thrushes are chirping in the nearby low-branched ginkgo trees. Michael helps me out of the truck, again taking my hand, as we walk toward the many food stalls.

"Let us get some food."

I select an egg salad sandwich with a pickle and slaw. Michael orders a loaded hot dog with sauerkraut.

We enter the town hall and take seats. He spreads a blanket on top of a bleacher near where the band will be playing. We eat in silence.

"Did you like the sandwich?" Michael asks.

"Yes, it was quite good as they added fresh dill weed to it. Did you enjoy the hot dog?"

"I sure did. It is hard not to like a hot dog."

Yes, I muse. I bet this is what you are – a non-adventurous eater. "Glad you did."

"Do you know most of the music they will be playing?" Michael asks me.

"No, I am afraid I do not, but I trust your judgement. I do not get to hear many bands, in fact, this is my first time. What should I expect?" I am surprised how excited I am to hear the band.

"The director of the band will welcome us and give a little introduction to each piece. He may even review the main instrument sounds to prepare us to be able to hear them during the concert. The band will perform, and if all goes well, the music will continue until an intermission. During the intermission we can stand, walk around, and get something more to eat and drink. When the concert is over, the director will appear once again to see how the audience liked the music. I think you will enjoy the show, but please let me know if you wish to leave early. I want the event to be pleasant for you."

Our conversation is interrupted by the band that begins with a rousing march, and a lot of bodies move to the beat. They play many songs before taking a break.

"Well, look who is here."

I quickly turn my head, as the voice sounds like Peter's. It is Peter. "Hi Peter."

"Hi June, and hi to your companion."

"Hi, I am Michael Wenger." Michael shakes Peter's hand.

"Pleased to make your acquaintance. I'm Peter Brandt. Are you enjoying the music? I sure am." Peter smirks at me.

"The band is good. They played some of my favorite songs. How do you two know each other?" Michael asks.

I start to reply, but Peter beats me to it. "I work at the Lehman's general store and June shops there frequently."

"I know Mr. Lehman was looking for help. I would have been interested had I not gotten a job at the bank," Michael states.

"You work at the bank; do you like it?" Peter asks.

"Well. I have only been there six months, but I am learning a lot and getting to meet a lot of the community."

"We need good people to take care of our hard-earned money!" Peter again peers my way and winks his one eye. "Listen, I need to get going. I work the late shift today. Good to see you and enjoy the rest of the concert." He shakes Michael's hand again and takes mine and kisses it. My world spins and I blush. This generates a titillating feeling unlike when Michael touched my hand.

"Peter seems like a nice guy," Michael says.

"Yes, he is helpful at the store." I think, indeed he is—more than nice.

As Michael outlined, the band director appeared before and after the show, and I enjoy the concert and the songs.

"Guess we should be getting you back home. It is about 3:30, and I want to get you home before 4 o'clock to score points with your father." We fold the blanket, dump our trash, and get back into the truck. Michael takes my hand to help me onto my seat; my body offers no reaction.

Chapter 30
Jealousy—January 1944

"June."

"Peter, what are you doing?" I am in the chicken coop gathering eggs. "You should not be here."

"I'm talking to you where no one can see. I need to talk with you."

"What is wrong?"

"What's wrong? Who is Michael, and what is going on between you two? I was so surprised to see you with him at the concert."

"Michael asked my parents for permission to court me. The band concert was our first official date."

"Well, I don't like this at all. It upsets me seeing you with him. It made me realize how much I care about you. I want to be courting you instead. I want us to date."

"You know it is impossible. You are not Plain. You cannot ask permission to court me. You and I cannot be together."

"Screw your religion. Sorry, but what do you want? Are you interested in Michael? It doesn't seem to me you are."

"I am trying to like him. I promised my parents I would try."

"Life is too short to try to fall in love. You can't make yourself do it. It happens. I don't know if I have fallen in love with you, but you have been on my mind constantly. I have enjoyed seeing you, and I want us to do more together."

"Peter, I am in a quandary. I do like what I know about you, and if I were a different person, I would like to date you. But I am who I am."

"And who exactly is that? Do you really know? From our conversations, I gather you want to see more of the world, and yet you are setting yourself up to remain on the farm if you marry Michael. Why court him if you don't have any feelings for him?"

"It is complicated. People of the Faith get shunned by their family and friends if they marry outside it. I cannot be seen with you in public without others judging me. If we were to date, I would need to be sure I am okay with leaving my religion. It is a lot to ask me to throw away."

"What would make it possible for us to spend more time together? Could I ask your father for permission to court you?"

"Absolutely not. Please do not ask him. He knows I am interested in you already and has told me he will forbid me to see you."

"He knows about us already and said he will stop us from dating? How did he find out?"

"Yes, he knows. I had a long chat with Mother about life and love. She perceived my attraction to you. She reminded me what I would lose if I persisted in liking you. She told Father. Soon thereafter, Michael's father asked Father for permission for Michael and I to court. I agreed. I figured it would lower my parents' concern about us. Do not get me wrong. I want to be with you, but I cannot."

"This is not acceptable. I need to see you, June. I want to see you. I must see you. If you have any desire to continue to see me, let's make plans on how to meet without anyone knowing, like we are now."

I am overwhelmed by the outpouring of his emotions. "I am so distressed, for I want to be with you—not Michael—but I need to keep courting Michael."

"Your loyalty to your parents is admirable. I'm trying to understand. Let's do this. I will leave you a note in the general store under a can of green beans on the back of the shelf. The note will list several places I think we can meet. If you agree, put a check beside them. Once we set the place, I will give you a time when I see you in the store. It may be coded, so others in listening range can't figure out what we are saying to each other. What do you think?"

"Peter, I can try. I do not know when I can get to the store."

"I will place the notes the days I work—Tuesday, Wednesday, and Saturday. Try to get to the store one of these days. I look forward to seeing your checked list. Thank you— you have given me hope for our future, as I do see one for us."

Chapter 31
Information Transfer—January 1944

"I am out of flour again. I should have had you get me a couple of pounds the last time. I need to go to the store again," Mother says.

"Can I go with you, Mother. I would like to buy a few needlework items."

"I guess you can, June, if Father can drop us off."

Today is Wednesday, and Peter should be working. I hide a pencil in my hem to be able to mark the list of potential meeting places. I need to remember to buy sewing notions, so Mother does not get suspicious.

As we enter the store, Mr. Lehman is the first to greet us. I do not see Peter. Mother orders two pounds of flour and a couple of other items. I meander the aisles and find the canned green beans. At the back of the shelf and under the last can, I see something white. I lift the can, grab the note, and place it in my dress apron. Mother does not see me do this luckily.

"Mr. Lehman, may I use the restroom," I ask.

"Sure thing, it's in the stockroom to the left."

I find the restroom, remove the pencil and note and check several locations among the nine offered. I think four will be safe; I prioritize them. Slipping the note and pencil back in my apron, I open the door to find Peter getting sugar out of the barrel and placing it in pound bags. I put a finger to my mouth, quieting him and handing him the note. I walk to the front of the store.

In a couple of minutes, Peter surfaces. "Hello Mrs. Davis and June. Happy to see you are getting more ingredients for baking. I love a good cookie or pie."

"Hello Peter. How are you today?" Mother inquires.

"Doing well, thank you, and you? Hello, June."

"I am fine. I ran short of flour and June wanted to come along to get some needlework notions."

Yes, the notions. I quickly scan the sewing aisle and sort through the threads to find a color I can possibly use in the future. I better get another color, so it seems I needed these notions. I take both spools to the register.

"I'll be happy to total your bill." Peter states.

"Yes, if you could put it on our monthly tab. June's items too. She is worth it." Mother replies.

"I couldn't agree more," Peter smiles at her and me. As we leave the store, Mother grins at me oddly. "You do like him; I can see it in your eyes and face."

Chapter 32
Rendezvous—January 1944

Today, Beulah and I are asked by our teacher to prepare a short story about a horse. Being a cold day, we decide to work on it near the school's fireplace. As she is writing, I hear a stone tap on the window. I look and Peter is standing behind an oak tree. He indicates he is placing a note under a rock and quickly disappears.

"May I read what you have written, Beulah?"

"Sure, give me additional ideas if you will."

"Will do, I am going to sharpen this pencil first; I will be right back." I quickly go outside to snatch the note Peter left under a rock indicating the location and time for our meeting. It is this Saturday morning at 9:30 at the stream behind our farm. This should be doable as the family does chores on Saturday morning. I will volunteer to do something that places me by the stream—like picking rose hips and wintergreen berries for tea. A quiver of excitement shoots through me as I think about seeing Peter again. I hope this works and we will not get caught.

It is the early hours of Saturday morning, and I am finding it hard to sleep, as I am so happy to be meeting Peter. Around

7:45, I get out of bed and put on an old wool dress, for the weather is cool. I eat oatmeal, grab a basket, put on a heavy shawl, and tell Mother "I am off to pick berries and hips for tea."

"Sounds good, June," Mother says.

Skipping for joy, I get to the stream on time and select a nice rock hidden in some trees. As promised, Peter arrives soon thereafter and finds me with a broad smile on my face.

"Dear June, you made it! Any trouble with getting out of the house?"

"No trouble at all, except I need to find some wintergreen berries and rose hips—my excuse for coming here."

"Let's sit first, and then we can look for them. I'll brush off this rock; we can sit here. I brought a blanket and almonds if you want any."

"You think of everything."

"I sure try."

"What are you going to do with the rest of your day?"

"I work this afternoon at the store. It should be busy, for today is a sale day at the hardware store. Folks wait for this day to gather more supplies for the winter. What about you?"

"I have started a good book. Once I finish the chores, I hope to read it with a cup of warm tea."

"Let's not waste this time on small talk. I want to ask you some questions and give me your first answer, okay?"

"I guess."

"What's your favorite color? Your favorite dessert? Your favorite thing to do?"

"Not fair; you asked me three questions, not one."

"Picky, aren't we? Well, start answering."

"Purple, cherry pie, and reading." Secretly, I am thinking being with you is fast becoming a favorite thing.

"You answered those questions pretty quickly."

"I did—now your turn."

"Blue, chocolate cake, and talking with you."

"No fair again…you have not talked with me often, so how can it be your favorite thing to do?"

"Like I said before, I know what I like, and I like you. I do have a favor to ask. I know within your family and community, your speech is very formal. It's not my style though. Please feel comfortable being more relaxed with me when we chat, ok?"

I give him a demure look and look at the ground. He lifts my chin with his hand. I look at him. He peers into my eyes, leans in and kisses my right cheek. I withdraw my chin to gaze at him. He reaches over and takes my right hand. "June, I don't want to scare you, but I would like to give you a kiss on your lips. Okay?"

I slowly nod and lean forward. He puts his warm lips on mine and gives me a quick peck.

"Not so bad, was it? I promise, June, I will never harm or hurt you. You are so refreshing. I love your innocence and integrity. I could sit here and kiss you more, but I want us to go slowly so you are not frightened. I want one more kiss now."

This time the kiss lasts longer with his lips staying on mine for what seems like glorious hours, and then he says "You better pick those berries and hips."

Chapter 33
We Meet Again—January 1944

All night I am restless recalling the feeling of Peter's lips on mine. Being such a strong man, how can he be so tender? When he kissed me, he seemed so soft and cuddly. I want to hold him and have him put his arms around me. I want to feel the warmth of his body against mine. I know I shouldn't have these thoughts, but I want him. See, I'm even changing my speech or thought patterns to match his. My understanding of love is becoming clearer. It's wanting to be with a person, to share daily experiences, to spend time alone together, to care so much about each other nothing else matters. I know these bodily thoughts are wrong, but I have them and can no longer deny them. I want to be loved, and I want to be loved by someone I want, not someone forced upon me.

A small stone hits the bedroom window. I look out and see Peter standing behind our one shed. He is motioning to me to come out for our second rendezvous. I motion I'll be out soon. I practically skip every other step on the stairway. Mother and Mary are in the kitchen.

"Morning, Mother and Mary. I am going to gather eggs."

"Do you want to eat first?" Mother asks.

"You all go ahead and eat. I will have leftovers when I return." I am anxious to get to Peter.

"Okay, if the leftovers are gone, you can make an omelet."

"I will find some food, do not worry about me." I grab the egg basket, throw on a shawl and exit via the back door.

My siblings greet me as they are coming inside to eat. Perfect timing, I think. They will all be eating and not be able to see Peter as I sneak into the woods.

"Man, don't you look pretty?" Peter says as he comes around the corner of the shed. "I love the color blue on you."

"Thank you, Peter. Let's get going before anyone has the chance to see us."

"In a hurry are ya, you must have enjoyed our last outing. And I noticed the use of a contraction—bravo!"

Demurely I look at him and smile. "You are starting to know me too well, Peter. I have thought of nothing else."

"It's a contagious disease, as I have thought about you nonstop. Let's go this way, as I think no window faces this direction."

It doesn't take long to get to the woods. We enter a bushy area with a lot of low-lying branches of trees and lots of ground cover. The smell of fresh peat permeates the air. A squirrel jumps from one limb to another for our entertainment.

"This fallen oak log can support both of us. I brought a towel. Let me lay it on the log before you sit so you don't get dirt on your dress."

"Peter, you are so kind."

"The towel is only the beginning, as I packed some peanut butter sandwiches. I figured you would be starving."

"I am. I told Mother I would eat when I return, but I am so hungry I could eat both this sandwich and breakfast later."

"Quite an appetite you have young lady. Is it only for food?"

My face turns scarlet. I can't look at Peter. I am so conflicted. I desperately want him to kiss me again. Who am I? I will burn in hell for this.

"Oh Peter, if thinking of you is hunger, I am starving. I cannot lie to you. I have thought of you and our kiss and nothing else. The way your lips touched mine so tenderly. I didn't know kissing could be so intoxicating. You have awakened emotions within me I never thought I could feel. You have created a beast."

"Music to the ears. I am delighted I made such an impact. But before I treat you with another kiss, let's find out more about each other. Ask me a question."

"Okay, give me a peek into your preferred life. Tell me what a perfect daily living scenario would be for you."

"First of all, you are in this scene front and center. Each morning, we wake up together, cuddle in bed before breakfast, share a pot of aromatic coffee and take turns making breakfast. We shower together and dress for the day. I go to work, and you could also if you want to. When we get home, we'll sit on the porch and have a refreshing drink (whatever kind) followed by a romantic candlelit supper we prepare together. I'll let you imagine what happens in the hours post supper."

For some strange reason, I am now able to look Peter in the eye. I peer at him, grab his hand, and say "You described my perfect scenario. I can't think of any better way to spend a day. I want to be with you Peter, I do. God help us to get through what we must to be together."

"I am overcome, June. Are you sure you are willing to risk it all? If so, I do want to talk with your father about courting you. Maybe he will see we are in love and bless us."

"You are a dreamer, Peter. Father will never give his consent. If you ask him, he will forbid me from seeing you."

"Let's not spoil our time hashing over what we can't control. Let's make the most of this day."

He leans in and kisses me on the cheek. I surprise him by returning his kiss, but not on his cheek. I don't pull away. I feel his tongue on my lips pushing them apart as it enters my mouth. Our eager tongues touch and circle around within our mouths. Peter turns towards me and puts his arms against my back, pulling me closer. His sandalwood smell intoxicates me. We kiss for what seems like eternity. This feeling is beyond wonderful. Peter pulls back.

"You better gather those eggs. I will leave the woods via this direction. You return the way you came. I will let you know of our next meeting place and time soon. Give me a parting kiss."

The parting kiss is another long one involving our searching and clinging tongues.

"June, you have my heart." Peter jumps and leaves me on the log. I can't move with my weak legs and racing heart. Who knows where my head is, as it isn't doing what it has been taught. Eventually, I compose myself and go to the chicken coop.

Chapter 34
Supper Preparations—January 1944

"Father and I thought it would be nice for you to invite Michael to supper so we can all get to know him better. I was thinking maybe Friday night would be good. Would this be okay with you, June?" Mother asks.

I look at her and reluctantly agree. At least I won't have to be alone with Michael. I can observe how he interacts with the family. "This sounds fine, Mother. Who will ask him?"

"I thought Father should as this would be only your second courting event. I do not want you to appear to be too forward."

"Okay, let Father issue the invitation."

Mother asks me to help prepare the meal, so Michael can see what a great cook I am. It is the last thing I want to do, except it might mean getting to go to the general store. As it's only Monday, there are two days I could possibly run into Peter if I can get to the store. "I will be glad to help plan and prepare the meal. Let me think about what a good menu would be." I plan to select dishes requiring a trip to the store.

"Perfect. Michael can get a glimpse of your terrific planning skills."

I get the recipe box out of the cupboard and begin to look for recipes. Mother seems pleased I am willing to have Michael over for supper. Little does she know the source for my enthusiasm—the hope I'll get to see Peter at the store.

It took me hours to go through the file to prepare a menu and share it with Mother.

"The menu is complete and sounds like it will suit most. There are dishes requiring ingredients we do not have on hand."

"I will prepare a grocery list and am glad to go to the store to purchase them."

"Good idea. I am sure Father will be going to town this week."

Before supper, I overhear my parents talking. At supper, Mother announces to the family that Father is going to invite a guest to supper for Friday night. Thomas snickers "I bet I know who it is."

"Since you are so wise, Thomas, who do you think is coming to supper?" Mother asks.

"I think it is June's new fellow, Michael. They seem to talk often at school."

"Thomas, be quiet," I say.

"June and Michael…June and Michael…," Thomas chants.

"Quite enough, Thomas. Eat your supper and leave June alone. When Michael is here for supper, I expect you to be well-behaved. It is important you do not scare him."

On late Tuesday afternoon, Father said he was going to swing by the Wenger's to ask Michael to supper. I ask if I can go along to get the supper ingredients afterwards at the general store. Father agrees.

I put on a nicer dress than what I had worn to school. I fix my hair and brush my teeth. Bouncing down the stairs, I announce I am ready to go.

Father appears from his room. "Let me have a cup of coffee first, and we will be on our way."

"I will be outside when you are ready." I need to work off some newfound energy. I might get to see Peter. I forget what hours he works on Tuesday, but I am hoping I will run into him. Let Father drink all the coffee in the world, as the later we get to the store, the better.

Father pulls into the Wenger's driveway. He slams the truck door and knocks on the front door. I can hear everything from the truck. Mrs. Wenger greets him. "To what do we owe this surprise visit?"

"I am here to ask if Michael would like to join my family this Friday evening for supper. We would like to get to know him better."

"Sounds fine to me but let me call Michael so you can ask him directly."

"Michael, there is someone here to see you."

"Hello, Mr. Davis. Is the family okay?"

"Indeed, everyone is fine. So fine, I am here to inquire if you would join us for supper this Friday evening. We think it would be a great way for us to get better acquainted."

"Friday evening? I cannot think of any conflict. I gladly accept. Thank you. May I bring a dish?"

"Just yourself. How does 5:30 sound?"

"Sounds perfect. Thank you. I will see you around 5:30 this Friday."

Father walks back to the truck, jumps on the seat, and says "He accepted."

As we pull away, I reposition myself on the seat. "Great." However, I am thinking not about seeing Michael on Friday but possibly seeing Peter soon. It is around 4:30 p.m.; I hope he is working.

Father goes with me into the general store. Peter is grinning at the front of the store. "Well, what a fine sight to see. How are you, Mr. Davis and June?"

"We are here to get some more cooking ingredients. Is Mr. Lehman around?"

"No, he has the day off," Peter says.

Since I cannot talk with Peter alone, I announce "We are having Michael Wenger over for supper Friday night and are here to buy items for the meal."

"Oh, I see," Peter says. "We just got some special herbs, but I haven't unpacked them yet. Will you come to the storeroom for a minute for me to show you?"

I go around the counter to the storeroom with Peter leading. Once we get there, he grabs my arm and pulls me toward him. He kisses me firmly on the lips.

"There, remember this kiss as you're eating supper. I am starting to love you so much, June."

I pull away and mutter, "And I you. I've been thinking about our situation and want to make a proposal."

"A proposal—for me? Isn't it supposed to be the guy who proposes to the girl?"

"You have surfaced a side of me I didn't know existed. I am tired of our rushed rendezvouses. What if I try and get away for a day so we can go somewhere, just the two of us?"

"Can you do that?" Peter asks. "Maybe skip school?"

"Skipping school is too risky as my siblings will observe my absence and tattle on me. It would be better if we escaped on a Saturday, as everyone is usually busy with farm chores. I'll say I'm to go to my friend's house for dinner followed by some group quilting. They live within walking distance of our farm. You can stop for me along the way. Would the Saturday after this one work for you?"

"There's no reason it shouldn't. I'll stop for you around 10 a.m. unless I hear otherwise."

"Wish me luck. I have never lied to my parents before; it won't be easy, but I want to spend time with you."

"And I with you. We better go back into the store."

Father gives me a strange look when we return. I show him the two herb plants Peter has given me in the storeroom. "June, are you ready to go?

"Could we get these plants? We can grow them inside until spring."

"Sure." Peter adds them to our tab. "Peter, take care," Father says.

"I will, Mr. Davis. You as well."

I gather the herbs as Father collects the rest of the goods. Father leaves first, so I glance behind me. Peter is waving and blows me a kiss. I melt inside.

Chapter 35
An Escape—January 1944

"Take these cookies along for the dinner at Sally's, June," Mother says. "It is so nice of her to invite you to her quilting bee. When do you think you will return?"

"It is hard to tell but my guess is before dark. I am not sure how long the quilting bee will last, so it is difficult for me to give you a specific time."

"Understand. You look nice in your wool dress. Give my best to all and do not forget your sewing basket."

"Got it right here. I think the bee will be fun. There may be other people there from school as well, I am not sure."

"Have fun and do not eat too much. I am going to keep your sisters busy polishing the furniture and mopping floors today."

"I am doubly happy to be going to Sally's with this news."

With my basket and cookies in hand, I walk toward Sally's house located close by. Lying to Mother was strange; I must remind myself of the end goal. Soon a truck slows behind me; it is Peter's.

"Need a ride, beautiful lady?"

"Only with a handsome man; oh, you'll do for sure."

Laughing, Peter reaches over and takes my hand in his. "You mentioned about going somewhere where we could be incognito. I'm thinking with the small size of this town, anywhere is not safe except for my place. It's not much to look at, but I brought food home from the store, and I could make us a decent dinner or lunch in my world. I see you have a bag of something—is it edible?"

"Mother wanted me to take cookies to the family I'm visiting, so you are in luck; the contents are indeed edible and delicious."

"Are you okay with going to my tiny apartment? I promise to be on my best behavior."

"Peter, if I didn't trust you, I wouldn't have suggested our meeting. Your apartment and promise sound great."

"The other advantage is it won't take all day to get to it so we will have more time to eat and chat."

"Sounds like a winning combination."

"Great, you might want to duck a little as we go through town in case anyone can see you through the windshield. My dream is for a day when we can be seen together and no one will care or comment."

"Peter, I hear you. I want to come back to this topic once we get settled at your place. My mind and heart have been active. I've come to some conclusions via all my musings."

"Now you're sounding very mysterious…musings and heart…hoping they go well together and in my favor."

"You're so funny."

"The day is going to be a beauty although cold. I'm glad I get to spend it with my beauty. Well, here we are. I'll pull around back and we can enter through the basement. Warning—my place is no palace."

"Don't worry. I won't judge."

"Guess you won't be needing your sewing basket after all. I do have some missing buttons you could fix if you want—just kidding."

"I'll leave it in the truck, but here are the cookies."

Peter fumbles with the key, but soon we climb stairs to the main floor, entering via the kitchen. The apartment is modest, neat and clean. Peter has done some prepping, as I can smell the sterile scent of a cleaning solution. The sun flows through the front windows over the sink making the kitchen nice and bright.

"Care for a pop?"

"Yes, I'd like one."

"You can hang your shawl on the hook in the hall if you want. I'll get the pops and then we can sit a little before I start preparing dinner."

Hanging my shawl, I glance around and see several doors off the hallway. "How did you find this apartment?"

"My Uncle Arthur gets credit for that. When my Dad told Uncle Arthur he wanted me to come help with the feed mill, my uncle inquired, and someone he knew owned this place. This man's mother, who recently passed, had lived here and he needed a tenant. I was the lucky guy."

"That worked out well for everyone it sounds like."

"Indeed. I feel a little guilty now that I have switched jobs to the general store, but my Uncle Arthur said he understands. He couldn't afford to pay me, and I needed cash for gas, rent, and food. Let's take our pops into the living room and sit."

The living room is not as bright as the kitchen as it faces a different direction. There are just a few pieces of furniture within it—a sofa, a couple of comfortable cushioned chairs and a coffee table. All are used, but they match in color and style. "Did you furnish the apartment," I ask.

"No, most items were already here. I bought the used coffee table at an estate sale. I had nowhere to place my food, as I often eat in here and not the kitchen."

There's a little discomfort on my part being in a man's house alone, but the feeling soon subsides as Peter starts talking about himself.

"This is my first time living away from my parents. I like the space and freedom it gives me to not have to answer to anyone."

"Are your parents difficult? Your moving to help your uncle versus staying and helping your father indicates some tension exists among you? True?"

"Tension is a good word. My dad wanted me to take over the butcher shop and the farm when he retired. My desires are different. I want to leave our small community and see parts of the world. I have always been interested in many things, and killing animals is not high on that list. People need to eat, I realize, but there must be more to life than taking it away from creatures one after another. It is hard to explain this to Dad without hurting his feelings, as that is what his life is about. He, of course, sees it from a different perspective, which I respect. Butchering is a means of making a living and providing for his family. He analyzed what the town lacked and concluded a local butchery would fill the gap. A small farm became available for him to purchase and suddenly, the entire family becomes volunteer help. Like you, I had my daily farm chores to do albeit on a reduced scale."

"So, you understand where I'm coming from Peter. Maybe that's why we get along so well. It's difficult to be raised into a life and then expected to keep it despite one's own druthers. I mentioned I have been thinking a lot lately about things. I give you credit for this. Previously, I thought nothing of staying in my current setting, my religion, and my proposed future of marrying someone of the Faith with the idea of starting a family. You have changed all of this. You have stirred hidden yearnings within me I didn't know existed. When I'm with you, I'm alive. Our lives should be what we want, not what others expect them to be. Peter, I am willing to leave my religion to be with you if you will have me."

"Wow, June. This is incredible news. My feelings for you continue to surprise me. You are a breath of fresh air to me as well. Together we could explore the world and create so much. In all my days, I have not met a woman who intrigues me the way you do. You bring out the goodness in me and give me hope. I can see a bright future together. Be careful though as your family will always mean a lot to you. If you were to marry me, you may lose contact with them. Are you okay with that? Think about it, as there is much to gain as well as lose if we go down this path together. I don't want you resenting me someday because loving me pulled you away from your family."

"If I decide to be with you, it will be my decision and mine to own. I want you to know I am falling in love with you and want to be with you."

"Oh, June. Thank you. This makes me beyond happy. I am falling in love with you also and have been from the first time we met. You fill a void within me beyond measure. We seem to complete each other."

"I feel so much better now I have shared my feelings with you." With that statement, a loud growl comes from my stomach.

"Sounds like it's time for dinner. I'll need help making sandwiches. Let's see how we work together in the kitchen. That will be a true test of companionship."

Chapter 36
Confrontation—January 1944

"Mr. Davis, may I have a few minutes of your time?" Peter asks as he approaches Mr. Davis in his barn.

"As you can see, I am feeding the horses, but I can stop and take a quick break. What can I do for you?"

"I have been an admirer of June's for a while. I think she is quite a wonderful woman, and I would like permission to date her."

"This is quite a surprise. I do not need time to think about this though. Are you of the Plain Faith?"

"No, Mr. Davis, I am not. I do believe in God though and think he has a special plan for each of us."

"Peter, I can only give permission for courting to men who are of the Faith."

"Could you please consider making an exception?"

"I really cannot. I would suggest you forget about June and look for other women to court. She would lose so much if she married a non-Plain man."

"I understand theoretically, but I like her and do not wish to harm her. She is a special woman with many talents and great values."

"Thank you for saying these kind things about June. Her Mother and I have raised her with the Faith and agree she is a great individual. I wish I could grant permission Peter, but unfortunately, I cannot. I must forbid you from seeing her. In fact, I will have to curtail her coming to the store to see you. She seems eager to shop lately. I think I am beginning to understand why. Do we have an understanding? You are not to court her."

"This is extremely disappointing, as I like June, and I think she likes me. If you change your mind, please let me know. Good day, Mr. Davis."

Chapter 37
Family Unrest—January 1944

"Rebekah, I need to talk with you."

"Okay, shall we go to the hearth?"

"No, I think we need to go to the shed." John heads outdoors. Rebekah follows him after grabbing a warm shawl.

"With the urgency, this must be serious," Rebekah says.

"Peter stopped by when I was feeding the horses."

"Peter, what did he want?"

"He wanted me to grant him permission to date June."

"What did you say?"

"The only thing I could. I forbade him. I told him June needs to date someone of the Faith; he admitted he was not."

"How did you leave things with him?"

"I told him I could agree June is a great woman, but he needs to stay away from her. I said I would curtail her going to the general store, as they have been seeing each other there. He was very disappointed with my response."

"Oh, John, I was afraid this was happening. When June talks about Peter, she glows. Her face lightens, and she almost floats with glee. Prohibiting them from seeing each other will not keep them apart. Love is strong, and they may sneak around behind our backs. We could see a much worse situation result."

"Rebekah, you know as well as I do, June cannot date a non-Plain man. She will be shunned if we allow her to do so."

"I know. This is awful. We might lose our daughter over this. What are we going to do?"

"Here is what we are going to do. We are going to talk with her right now. Where is she?"

"She is upstairs working on schoolwork I believe. Let me go see."

"I will wait here in the shed."

"June, are you here?" Mother asks as she climbs the stairs.

"Yes, Mother."

"May I come in?"

"Yes, Mother, the door is open."

Mother's face looks worried. "What is wrong, Mother. You do not look good."

"Please come to the shed with me. Father and I need to talk to you."

"Let me finish this sentence and meet you there." I have no idea what this is about, but I can tell it is not going to be good. I wonder if Michael has decided not to come to supper.

"June," Father says. "Peter stopped by today and asked me if he could court you."

"He did what? I am so surprised. What did you say?"

"The only thing I could. He affirmed he is not of the Plain Faith, so I told him he could not see you. It would cause too much harm to you and us. We would be shunned and thrown out of the meetinghouse."

I stand stiff and stunned. I cannot believe Peter went against my wishes. I told him not to ask my father for permission. Now, I will not be able to ever see him again.

"Furthermore, I have decided you can no longer go to the general store. You have been too eager lately to go for groceries. I told Peter—and I am telling you—you will not go to the store while he works there."

Now I am shocked. I want to scream how dare you, but I know Father is doing what he must. I have to see Peter again. It will break me. Overcome with emotion, I rush up the stairs, hearing Father calling me. I do not stop. I close and lock the door. I need privacy. I need Peter. I am so distraught. My life is ruined. I lay down on the bed and cry into the pillow. Life is so unfair. I did not ask to be Plain; I was born such. Maybe I need to suffer the consequences and leave home. Maybe Peter would be willing to run away with me. We would be together. I need to see him to ask if he is willing.

Mother comes to see me. I request she go away. She persists. I reluctantly open the door and let her enter. She hugs me as tears fill her eyes.

"June, please understand we know how hard this decision of Father's is on you. I can tell you love Peter. I am conflicted. I want you to be happy, as you have been a wonderful daughter, but I do not want you hurt by your actions. Dating Peter would mean you would have to leave us and your friends. You would have to start over somewhere else with someone you know very little about. Peter seems nice, but you two have not spent a lot of time together to know if you would last forever. Again, I suggest you pray about this and perhaps have a talk with the bishop about what options would be available if you do decide to date. More information may lead to clarity."

"I need to take a walk by myself to think about this, but I will be back before supper."

"Please do return and be careful. You are in a poor state of mind—stay alert."

I reach for a shawl and descend the stairs before any of my siblings see me. Rushing to the woods, I walk blindly. What can I do? I should not contradict my parents, but I do not want to marry someone I am not in love with. I have experienced what love feels like, and it is not what I feel toward Michael. I need to talk to Peter. Wait, I may be able to find him at the store, as it is Wednesday afternoon. I retrace my steps and walk along the driveway into town. Father is not going anywhere today, and if I see anyone else, I will say, I am running an errand. I must see Peter.

Luck is with me, because I do not see anyone on the walk into town who knows me. I cannot go into the store if Mr. Lehman is working. He would tell Father I stopped. I peek in the window by the counter and see Peter completing a sale. I wait until he is finished and throw a small stone at the window. This gets his attention. He seems surprised to see me and shakes his head he cannot come out. I plead with him with my facial expression to please reconsider. Soon, I hear him tell Mr. Lehman he is going to get wood for the stove and will take his break while he is doing so. He appears immediately.

"What are you doing here, June?"

"We need to talk. Father told me you asked his permission to date me, and he told me I can no longer see you even here at the store. I asked you not to ask him, why did you?"
"Seeing you with Michael was hard. I thought maybe there would be a chance your father would give me permission."

"Well now, we are forbidden to see each other. I need you and want you, but I can't have you. I don't know how to go on without you. I want us to be together so much! In fact, I am ready to suffer the consequences of leaving the Faith and want to let you know. I need to be able to see you, Peter. Life without you if unthinkable."

"Wow, June, please think about this some more. While I'm pleased you want us to be together, think about what all you will leave behind. Be sure you want to part with your family and friends. I need to get back to work. Let's take a little break from each other and think about what we both want. I'll check back with you to see what you have decided. I'll swing by the school and leave you a note again under a stone by the oak tree. I do love you and want the best for you. Please think about what you want meanwhile."

Peter gives me a peck on the cheek and returns to the store. I walk home very sad and in a daze that Peter wants a break, not caring if anyone sees me. My world is ending as far as I am concerned.

Chapter 38
Seeking Guidance—January 1944
Peter

"Mom, Hello. How are you and Dad doing there in Georgia?" Peter inquires, telephoning his mother from the general store.

"What a pleasure it is to hear your voice. Your Dad and I miss you tremendously. Well, I do. Dad won't admit it, as he can be so stubborn. I really wish the two of you would come to terms and pocket your pride. He loves you but is disappointed you didn't want to take over the butcher shop. He had a plan in his head he failed to share with you until it was too late. You had already moved on with your life and didn't want to stay here and make the store transition. I understand, but Dad is having a tough time. He thought if you went away for a while, you might change your mind. Any hope of that?"

"Sorry, Mom. I haven't altered my stance. In fact, I have gotten a paying job, so I am no longer helping Uncle Arthur with his feed mill."

"What are you doing instead?"

"I'm staffing a general store. I meet all kinds of people and am not living under someone's thumb all the time. I can try new things, arrange displays, suggest ideas for improvements, all of which are welcomed. It's quite a change."

"I am glad to hear your voice. You sound happy. I'm sorry things were tense between you and Dad when you left."

"Well, to be honest, they have always been. Our feelings just intensified when I told him I wanted to move on to a different life."

"Yes, you are right. I still regret the hard feelings harbored between you two."

"I know. You have been my anchor. In fact, do you have time to talk? I have something that's bothering me, and I'd like your advice."

"Sure, what is it darling?"

"I've met a girl who means the world to me."

"That's wonderful, Peter. Tell me about her."

"Her name is June Davis and she's a customer at the store. She lives on a farm with her big family of nine and is about to graduate from high school."

"What's she like?"

"She's incredible. She's a mixture of true humbleness, kindness, and innocence. She works hard to help her mother with household chores and with caring for the other members of the family. She is very smart and has a warm personality. She is shy when you first meet her, but her genuine warmth radiates once you get to know her."

"Is she pretty?"

"Well, she is not tall nor petite. I guess that makes her about average height. She has golden brown hair and dark brown eyes. She's slim but not too skinny. You'd like her."

"How did you meet her?"

"She needed help with carrying some goods from the store to meet her father at the feed mill. My manager asked me to help her. Mom, I don't know why, but I was attracted to her from that moment on and continue to be even more so every time I see her. I think you would really like her."

"I've never heard you talk this way about any girl before. It sounds like you are smitten. When did you begin dating?"

"That's the thing. I really haven't."

"Why not?"

"It's because she is Plain. I just learned what this means. Plain is a type of religion similar to the Amish or Mennonites, but it is more liberal. They drive cars that are all black. They work within the English world, but they stick together to support their beliefs and traditions. June's faith doesn't permit her to court a man outside of it. I obviously am not Plain"

"Oh my, I see. This is complicated. I'm not well versed with the Plain religion."

"I tried to ask her father for permission to court her and was denied. The family is so formal and stoic with each other, even with their speech. She is currently being courted by someone her family encouraged her to date. She is miserable because she doesn't like him romantically. It's tearing me apart seeing her so unhappy. She says she likes me, but she can't date me without her father's permission. Mom, I am beside myself. I want to be with her so much, but I am prohibited from seeing her officially. We share clandestine meetings in the woods behind her house or around the farm sheds and sometimes at her school. I used to see her when she came into the store, but now her father won't let her shop after I asked him about courting her. I'm going crazy, Mom."

"I can hear the struggle in your voice. It sounds to me like you need to forget her and move on. You will never be accepted into the family and if she is as obedient, as it sounds like she must be, you won't be able to win her over. She'll have to defy her parents in order for that to happen. It's best you just leave her alone and find someone else."

"Oh Mom, I was afraid you were going to say this. While my mind agrees with you, my heart is telling me this is true love and worth the fight. I feel like I'm not going to win though, and I will need to find a solution for my angst. I never thought love would be this hard."

"Peter, I wish I was there to give you a big hug. Be happy you have feelings of this magnitude as many people never do. I'm so sorry they are for someone who's not able to reciprocate. You need to move on and let her do the same."

"Thanks for the advice, Mom. I hope you have a good weekend. I'll try and get home soon. I miss you so much."

"It'd be wonderful to see you. Call me again if you need me. I'm always here for you and am one of your biggest fans."

"Love ya, Mom."

"Love you too, Peter. Bye."

Chapter 39
Supper is Served—January 1944

Thursday, Mother and I start baking for tomorrow's supper. I realize my quietness is bothering her, but I cannot help it. I am dreading seeing Michael. I am such a hypocrite. I know I will never care for him the same way I do about Peter.

"You are thinking, June. If you want to share, you know I am here to listen."

"Thanks, Mother, but I have few words to share. My heart is heavy, and I am extremely sad."

"I can see sorrow in your eyes. I will not make you talk, but sometimes things become clearer if you do."

"Sorry, Mother, not today."

Supper includes pork roast, potatoes, cooked cabbage, roasted carrots, fresh-baked rolls, and apple pie for dessert. Mother is rolling the dough for the pie as I pare and cut apples into slices. We have mixed and kneaded the rolls, and they are rising a second time. The smell of yeast is strong. Both the pie and rolls will be baked in the wood-fired oven tomorrow. I will wash the carrots tonight and chop the cabbage.

Tomorrow, I will come home early from school to help with the rest of the meal. Mother will cook the roast in the morning, so the meat will be extra tender. My younger sisters will help to set the table and steam the vegetables.

Friday night comes before I am ready. The table is set as is the meal. There is a knock at the door, right on time—5:30 p.m. Father opens the door and welcomes Michael. He hangs his jacket on the hall hook. Father says, "Come on in Michael. You know everyone I believe." Father proceeds to introduce my siblings, ending with me. "And of course, you know June. Rebekah, Michael is here."

From the kitchen, Mother enters the room to say hello and asks if Michael would like an iced lemonade. He accepts. I ask for one as well. Mother returns with a tray of glasses and distributes them.

"What is new, Michael?" she asks.

"Not a whole lot. I have been working at the bank as a teller."

"Wonderful, Michael," Father says. "I bet you meet a lot of members of the community."

"True, it is a great opportunity to learn more about the people who live and work nearby."

"How long do you plan to work at the bank?" Father asks.

"I hope to work for several years and become a loan officer. I want to help our neighbors achieve their dreams."

"That is quite a laudable goal," Mother says. "I think supper is ready, so family, take your usual seats at the table, and Michael, please take the remaining seat."

Conversation continues throughout the evening as we eat, but my contributions are minimal, and my head is elsewhere. I do not care about Michael's goals and dreams. I do not see myself being a part of them. I cannot force myself to be hospitable. My parents make questioning gestures as they try to encourage me to be actively involved in the chatter. I just cannot engage. This is someone else's life; it is not my future. I want out and vow to remove myself, whatever the cost.

Chapter 40

Surprise Direction—January 1944

Several days pass, and I have not seen Peter anywhere. Running into him is impossible, as I am not permitted to go to the general store. To make matters worse, I am required to sit with Michael during services, due to our official and public courting. Nothing upsets me more than having to be by Michael's side. The chains around me are tightening, and I am trapped like a wild animal. Duty becomes my middle name. My parents observe me closely as I am moody, and for me, belligerent. I spend a lot of time alone in my room. I want to escape the situation I am in.

Some clothes need mending, so I am alone in my room sewing on a button when a stone hits the window. Could it be Peter? I rush to see, and indeed, he is standing behind a tree. He motions I come to him. I indicate I will be right there. I grab a shawl from a wall hook and go downstairs. As luck would have it, no one is around. Falling into his arms, he pushes me away. I am stunned. Why is he not hugging me?

"June, we need to talk. Let's go into the woods."

"Peter, what's happening? You seem distracted." He doesn't answer but takes me gently by the arm and leads me into the wooded area behind our house. Again, we sit on a log, this time one from a downed oak tree. Sow bugs curl as we disturb their peace.

"June, I have missed you so much. I know I'm forbidden to see you, but I need to tell you this in person."

"What is it, Peter?"

"If I can't be with you, I don't want to stay here. Being around this area, I am constantly reminded of you. I can't have you throw away your life for me, either. You deserve better. So, I came to tell you I have enlisted with the army and am reporting to boot camp in a couple of weeks. I have been feeling guilty about not fighting for our country, as it appears Hitler is infiltrating more European countries. My friends have already joined and are fighting in Europe. We need to stop him before he conquers Europe and us. I am going to North Carolina to Camp Butner soon."

My thoughts are muddled, and no words exit my lips; I am speechless. Tears swell and fall as my body begins to shake. I feel betrayed once again. How could he do this without asking me?

"June, are you okay? You're quiet."

"Hold me."

Peter pulls me toward him and puts his arms around my trembling body. "I knew this would be a shock, but it's the only answer to our problem. I can't stay here, and you can't go with me. We need to distance ourselves. We need to forget about each other. You need to court Michael. Promise me though, you won't marry him unless you fall in love with him. Your ultimate happiness is what I want."

"Why didn't you ask me before you enlisted?"

"Because I knew you would try to talk me out of it. This is the only way I can survive without you—I need to get away and start a new life."

"But what about your job and family?"

"Mr. Lehman told me he can hire someone else. He respects my wanting to fight to save our country. He even gave me a severance to help me with expenses during boot camp. He's a decent person. As for my family, my siblings can help with the butcher shop. And if Father needs more help, he can hire someone. It doesn't take talent to staff the shop."

"Will you ever come back to me?"

"I doubt it angel, as it would be hard for me to see you with someone else. Trust me, this is the best solution for all of us. Know though I love you and want only the best for you.

You are my first love and will always retain a special place in my heart. I wish our story ended differently; I do." He embraces me and kisses me on the lips for the last time.

I can't stand it. I force my body out of his grip and run to the house to throw myself on my bed. This time, I don't even try to hide my tears or my crying. This is the worst thing I have experienced. Being a good girl has not paid off. Love is terrible if this is what one feels when one's heart is broken. Why is God punishing me? I cry until I fall asleep and only wake when I smell the scents of supper; they make me nauseous.

"Are you okay June?" Mother asks. "Supper is almost ready; I need the table set."

"I have an upset stomach. Go ahead and eat without me tonight."

"Sorry you are not feeling well. I will reserve some supper for you, so come down when you feel better."

"Thanks, Mother." I hurt so badly, I cannot imagine the day when I will be hungry again.

Chapter 41

Community Support—February 1944
Peter—Camp Butner, North Carolina

I've been in North Carolina now for several weeks. I have met great guys from all over the country. My body aches in places I never knew existed. Our training is very intense, and we are always under strict rules. I'm learning obedience like I never thought possible. It's "Yes Sir" this and "Yes Sir" that, always with a quick salute of the hand. I am a lowly private among senior officers who need to dominate. Our beds must be made just so, and our boots are to be polished beyond shiny. We exercise at least eight hours a day. Meals are frequent, but the food is lousy. I miss Mom's home cooking. I also miss June terribly. Other guys get letters from their family and girlfriends. They share news when possible. I see how the letters from the girls help the guys stay positive and upbeat. They can be in a terrible mood; but once a letter arrives, they beam with joy. I wish June could write to me. But why would she? I had to run off to protect her, I hope she realizes this. Mom was right. There is no way a romance between us could have worked. Her world and mine would both have needed to change dramatically. While I know I did the honorable thing, my heart is breaking. I miss her so much. She is all I think about. It saddens me to think she doesn't even know the depth of my longing for her. I wonder if she has been able to move on and find happiness either with Michael or a new beau. I'm evil to hope she hasn't. I only want the best for her though.

"Mail call. Peter, looks like there are a couple of letters for you today."

"Great."

My heart jumps—could one be from June? Alas, no. They are from my brother and fellow soldiers. It's nice folks haven't forgotten about me. I should be grateful and read them. Heck, maybe I'll even respond.

Camp Wheeler
Macon, Georgia
February 17, 1944

Hiyi Pvt.,

How are you getting along without any stripes?

I am O.K. & I hope you are the same.

How do you like to drive the jeeps? Fine I hope.

Talking about hard days. We are getting them now. About three hrs. P.T. [physical training]. It sure is a bitch.

We have some kind of stuff they call "Judo". They teach you how to break a man's back, arm, or what ever you want to break.

Yesterday morning we went on a eight mile run. I mean a run. We ran about ¾ of the way. It was pretty tough.

Say you haven't seen any thing yet when you are talking about swamps. Wait until you get into Fla. Or Ga. Fla. is the ass hole of the U.S.

It has been raining a lot down here lately & the dam tents shrink & pretty near pull out the tent pins.

Last night I fell a sleep & either drop a cigarette or some fire off of it on my fatigues on the floor. It burnt them up & ruined a pair of shoes. So I guess I'll have some stuff to pay for.

This outfit is really getting hot. They are sure getting ready for something & I think it is a boat ride.

Have you gotten your furlough yet, or does it seem like you are going to get it? You ought to be able to go home on a three-day pass. I believe I could make it if I was allowed.

It is sort of hot around here too, but not as bad as Fla.

Well, I'll have to sign off as it will soon be time for another lecture.

So Long & Good Luck

David

(Write)

P.S. The whole south is hell.

— ∞ —

Fort Cluster, Michigan

February 21, 1944

7:45 am

Hi Peter,

How the heck are you? Getting much? I'm O.K. Well Peter how do you like the Army by this time? We finished our basic 2 weeks ago, but we still go on a few short hikes but mostly convoy work.

Last week, they cut each co. in our Regt. in half. They took the fuck ups and put them in the 513th. Q.M. Regt. Paul Miller is in the 513th but I am still in the 466th. I don't know how the hell they missed me.

Well Peter is Boob still with you or are you separated? We got foot lockers yesterday. I think we are getting ready to move soon, in a couple of weeks.

How is the weather down there? It is cold up here and has been for several weeks. It snowed yesterday morning some but is all gone now.

Have you been on the Range yet? We go on the Range for anti-aircraft fire this afternoon or tomorrow.

I am going to try and get a 3-day pass tomorrow night but I don't think it will work for the captain said he didn't like to give them when we're moving soon.

Well Peter, I must close for we will be falling out for exercises soon.

So Long Until

Pollard

P.S. We see a good many movies or training films. If you get the chance to see "Kill or Be Killed" see it for it is dam good.

The reason I want a 3-day pass is since you are gone maybe the women are suffering. Do you think so, but I doubt it huh. "Ha ha"

— ∞ —

Decatur, GA

Feb 18, 1944 10:25

Hello Peter,

I will just drop you a few lines to let you know that we are all well and hope you are the same.

Mom and them expect to be done in there today with the tomatoes. Pop's going to try to get a job over the winter in there.

We are having some rain now. It started on Thursday and is still looking like we'll have some more. Cousin Clarence drilled a well down home. Well Pop helped pay for it and Amos bought a farm back of Clarkston, about 5 miles from Decatur. I guess you heard David is home on a furlough. He has to go back tomorrow night. He had to take two shots while he's home and two more when he goes back. He expects to get P.O.E. He said if he goes over seas he'll be rating pretty good with Staff Sarg. rating. He didn't get it yet, but the way he talked, he might get it pretty soon.

Paul was home last week after his ship was torpedoed, on a 72 hr. pass. I guess he was really scared. Knocked him clear out of bed and across the room. I bet he wishes he'd be on land now. It is raining now. The ground is pretty well soaked and the water's running in the gutters, as we are having a pretty nice rainy season. I guess you are up at the Motor Pool by this time but will be heading for Durham this afternoon. I want to go in to see "This is the Army." It's on in town. It is supposed to be good. By gosh it's starting to lightning. The thunder rattled the window panes. Ross Faust bought that wood down here at gate 8. It was but 7 now, about 80-90 loads in there. He bought Jake Hepfer's lot down there toward the school house to put it in. Well, that's all and so long and don't forget to write and not work too hard. Amos Bender, I think has a carbuncle on his ass.

Your Brother

February 27, 1944

Dear David,

I got your letter the other day but this is the first time I have had time to answer it. I was glad to hear from you and hope you are getting along all right now. I sure did not get any stones in any of my beans yet, but you can expect anything in here.

I am sorry to hear that all you have is swamp and mud but that is the way all new camps are. We have all concrete and macadam walks & roads here. I don't know how far I am from Camp Wheeler, but I guess 3 or 4 hundred miles.

We have had 7 weeks of basic training; we are in a 13-week cycle and boy it sure is tough. We have been on 16-mile hikes. We make it in 4 hrs. Mon. we start on nite problems and will do most of our work at nite.

I passed the mental test for the Air Corps the other week and expect to take the physical this week. I sure hope you do not have to carry full field pack for they sure get heavy. We carry ours all the time and rifles M.I. Well, you were lucky to get closer home. You should only be about 400 miles from NC. Well, take it easy and keep your nose clean; maybe we'll get to see you some day.

Pvt. Peter

P.S. I still like the Army all right. Write when you get time but you won't have much time if you get it like us.

Chapter 42
Time Stands Still—February 1944
Reading, Pennsylvania

Life becomes a blur. Michael and I court several times with the same outcome. His desire to progress with our relationship is met with no enthusiasm on my part. I go through the motions like a ragdoll—limp and expressionless. There is no way I can marry Michael, as my heart is still with Peter. I worry about what Peter is going through in boot camp. I cannot ask others if they have heard from him, as I am to be completely disassociated with him. Life is dull and my moods swing from mellow to despondent. There are days I barely make it out of bed. Today is one of those days.

"June, it is Mother. May I come in?"

"I guess."

"How are you feeling?"

"Not well." I answer in a short manner.

"What is hurting?"

"To be truthful, my heart is broken. I have thought this over and I cannot continue to court Michael. I would rather remain single than marry him. It is not fair to him for me to act like I am interested, when I am not. He needs to be released so he can find another woman to court. I can no longer maintain this façade."

"June, it has not been long since Peter left for boot camp. He did the respectable thing and removed himself from your life so you could get a fresh start as well."

"Respectable is not what I would call his behavior. He left me high and dry. Can you not tell I am miserable and unhappy?"

"Yes, we all see a difference in you, but again, give it time. The heart has a magical power of renewal. After more months, you will not feel so hurt or lost. Heartbreaks are tough, but they can mend over time."

"But I do not want to mend, I want Peter. He makes me complete. Without him I am worthless and distraught."

"You are not the first woman to experience a lost love, and you will not be the last. How about I request a session with the bishop for you?"

"Please, no. He will encourage me to marry Michael. I am telling you now, I will not do so. I would rather be dead."

"June, please, do not be so dramatic. Death is not an option. If you are seriously thinking of killing yourself, I need to take action. Suicide means going to hell. Please do not even think about this, please."

"It is a figure of speech, Mother. I am not considering suicide. Please tell Father I refuse to marry Michael; Michael needs to be told."

"I will talk with Father, but you need to give this more time before anyone talks with Michael."

"Okay, but I refuse to go on any more outings with him as of today. Let him get the message if you do not want to tell him directly; however, it seems like a more Christian approach to inform this kind man of my lack of interest."

Shaking her head, Mother gives me a hug and goes downstairs.

Chapter 43
Ecstasy—Late March 1944

Time passes, and I feel no different. Peter is all I think about. I yearn to hear from him. I want to be with him forever. My parents have gotten the message about Michael; we have stopped courting. I do not know what was said, but I do know the bishop participated in the conversation between the two fathers. I do not care. A woman should not be forced into a relationship, regardless of its convenience.

To add to my depression, the winter weather has been brutal. There is more snow this year than in the last three years combined. The animals are brought into the barn for fear of them freezing. Hay is getting low, as grazing on any remaining grass is impossible with the snow. The house has been cold, reflecting my demeanor. I am glad spring is almost here, as it represents new beginnings.

I have almost finished school and will graduate in May. Most of my classmates have paired and marriage is their next milestone. Michael found someone else to court and seems happy. Everyone seems happy except me. Life has become extremely dull and boring. Since I refuse to be courted, I am doomed to become a spinster who will remain with and care for her parents in their advanced age. This is what my future holds? It could have been so different.

A stone thrown at my window arouses me. Could it be Peter? Springing to the window, I see him behind a tree. I wipe my eyes, as I fear they are deceiving me. He gives me his usual wave to call me outside.

I am lucky, as the rest of my family is sitting around the fire playing games. They have gotten used to me not participating in family activities. I quietly slip down the stairs and exit via the back door.

Peter leads me to the barn. He motions for me to be quiet until we arrive in the hay mow. The smell of stale hay enters my nostrils. I feel the bounce return to my step and my blood flows once again. My body is alive—I haven't felt this way since he left for boot camp.

"Peter, I can't tell you how great it is to see you. I have so much to share about what has happened since you left."

"My sentiments exactly, June. You are a part of me wherever I go. I can't forget you as much as I try. I had to see you and am glad we can talk. Tell me what has been happening to you."

"When you left, I told my parents I would not court Michael any longer. I wasn't being fair to him, as I had no interest in marrying him. He should find another woman to court who would revere and cherish him. I haven't courted anyone since him. In fact, I told my parents I will stay with them to become their caregivers when needed. I have no interest in any other man. I can't Peter, as you control my heart. What's your news?"

"Boot camp has been tough, no doubt about it. We exercise all day long and learn fighting techniques. I've learned how to shoot guns—not a favorite thing to do. Many of the other men in the camp are from the southeast. I've made new friends and learned how to respect the officers. I'm proud to be serving our country; however, I don't see this as a career. How do they say—it's not my cup of tea?"

"How long are you home?"

"That's why I need to see you. I'm home for only a brief time. In two days, I fly to England. Since I'm trained, I will be deployed to the front lines of battle. Reality is setting in; I'm going to war. I couldn't leave without contacting you to see how you are handling my absence. Now that I know how you have been feeling, I have a proposal for you."

"I don't know what to say. I wish you weren't going to war. Be careful, as I can't have you getting hurt. I love you too much."

"So glad to hear this. I love you too, so very, very much. Getting hurt is not on my 'to do' list either. I want to live. I want to live because I want to come back and get you. In my many musings, I see us together permanently. A future as a parental caregiver is not what I want for you. I want us to be together. I'll come back and we'll get married and create a home together."

I didn't let him finish. I kiss him passionately. He pushes me away and gazes deeply into my eyes. A nod indicates he has my permission.

"Are you sure you want to do this? Maybe the talk of marriage has gone to your head?"

"Stop talking and love me."

He pulls a blanket from his backpack and spreads it on the hay.

"Always prepared I am, the ultimate boy scout."

"Didn't I say stop talking?"

"Getting bossy, are we?"

My kiss quiets him. He lays me on the blanket and grabs burlap sacks hanging on the hay mow side walls. "We can use these if you are cold." He proceeds to kiss my lips, neck, and ears. I reach around his neck to pull him closer. By this time, I have lost all sense of time and space. My body is on fire, and I am floating above it. Peter begins to loosen the ties on my apron front or bib, pressing a gentle kiss to my bodice. I push the sleeves on his jacket down his arms. He tosses it aside. He turns me on my side and unbuttons my dress. I shrug my shoulders to push the top of it to my waist. He tries to remove my slip but fails, so he lowers the straps. The breast covering is still intact. Peter pulls to lift it over my head. I am half naked for the first time in front of a man.

"Are you sure you want to do this, June. Once you have sex, there's no going back."

"I'm more than sure. I want you so badly."

With my breasts exposed, Peter kisses each nipple and sucks on them like a baby. An unrecognizable feeling transports through my body. It is a shooting pain; a delightful one. A foreign one. He presses his torso against my breasts and rocks me back and forth.

"June, you are more beautiful than I could have dreamed. I love you so much!"

He stands and removes his belt and pants. Standing before me in his boxers, he appears to be so tall. Boot camp has helped to shape his muscles. He is incredibly handsome. Returning to my side, he drops my slip and dress, until I am only wearing underpants.

"There's soon no point of return; I want to be absolutely sure you are okay doing this?"

"Hush and continue handsome man."

"Music to my ears."

Peter smothers me in kisses moving from my lips, to my decolletage, to my breasts. His finger circles around my one breast, as he sucks on the other. My body lifts and squirms as it reacts to these enticing touches. He takes my one nipple in his fingers and squeezes it. I scream.

"Quiet, we don't want to wake the animals or alert the family. But I hope your scream was one of joy. Let me know if I am too rough."

Peter removes my underpants by moving one side down, then the other, until they are at my ankles. I shake them off and am completely naked. I thought I would feel uncomfortable in such a state, but I find I am at ease. Sex is natural, after all. I understand why it is forbidden before marriage in our Faith. One would want to do it all the time otherwise.

I reach to lower Peter's boxers and am amazed at how easily they slide over his slender hips. Men don't have the rounded hips like women. The boxers catch in the front; I lift them over his penis. Now, he is naked as well. I see his enlarged penis and shut my eyes.

"Too much to look at?"

"No, it's so big. How will it go inside me?"

"I have ways, young miss."

Peter drops to my crotch and uses his fingers to spread my private parts. He lands on a spot making me shiver with delight. He rubs it gently in a circular motion.

"This my love, is the magic button leading to intense pleasure."

"Don't stop," I hiss.

Peter continues to rub and drops to use his tongue to massage the spot. This results in an indescribable earth-shattering sensation. I arch my back and muffle a primal sound. He grabs my nipples and pinches both as he continues to lick my crotch. My scream gets louder, so he stops.

"Keep going," I moan.

"Listen to me. Soon I will be entering you, as I can't wait much longer. This may hurt as this is your first time. You may bleed a little afterwards. All is to be expected. I will be gentle but let me know if it hurts too much."

I pull him back on top of me. He lifts his hips and again parts the skin in my crotch with his fingers to find the hole. I feel his warm tissue against mine. He pushes ever so gently. There is some pain, but nothing diminishes the ecstasy I experience being this close to him. Being coupled to Peter brings me joy. The pushing gets a little more frequent and the pain gets a little more intense, but not to a degree I want Peter to stop. The pushing stops and Peter begins to move in and out of my privates. I feel the rub inside and the heat. The movement gets more rapid and Peter screams. Fluid slowly streams down my legs.

"Are you okay?"

"More than okay; incredible. Thank you for being so kind. I can see how this could get addictive."

"I know. Unfortunately, this will be the only chance we have to make love until I return. I hope you will remember it fondly, and know we can do this every day, if we want, once I get back from the war. You are my angel, my love, and my reason for living. I love you so much."

"And you are my one and only love, Peter. You better return. I need you!"

"Here, let me help you wipe your legs, so you can put clothes on. Soon someone will discover you are absent."

Once dressed, we climb down from the hay mow and look in the window to see the family still intact in the living room. Peter plants one last long kiss on my lips.

"Remember this night until eternity. You are my North Star and my reason for being."

He runs into the woods, and I quietly creep upstairs forever changed, having experienced true love.

BOOK II

Chapter 44

Discovery—2016

Jean Pugh Shipman

Over fifty years have passed since I heard the kitchen conversation between Mother and Marion. I had forgotten all about it. Mother passed in 2015. While going through her things in preparation for an estate sale, I discovered a box of old letters. I started to pitch them when I noticed what appeared to be feminine handwriting with date stamps of 1944 on the envelopes, around the time the elusive cousin would have died. Reading them, I quickly determined they were written by the cousin; I had a first name! I didn't have time to read all of them as there were over 25 letters. Unfortunately, I know I tossed some before realizing what treasure I had found.

About a year later, I read the letters and got lost in a time warp. I traveled back to 1944 and was able not only to identify the cousin but to also determine she died when she was 25 years old. Mother's side of the family has books about their ancestors and family trees penned by family members. I searched through the family tree and found one single entry for a single woman who died at 25. No explanation was given for the early death; in fact, the entry simply stated her birth and death dates. This had to be her; the cousin who died prematurely. The first names matched as well. I proceeded to read all the letters I had saved, including ones from her to her parents, from her aunt to her mother, and from those around her during her time in New York City.

Chapter 45

Renewal and Hope—April 1944
Reading, Pennsylvania

It is spring, a sense of rebirth is rejuvenating me. I have experienced a part of nature, a forbidden part, but a fantastic one. My walk once again has spirit. My family notes my happier demeanor and is relieved I am no longer majorly depressed. They have no idea of the reason for my joy. They assume with the passing of time, my thoughts for Peter have diminished, and I have resolved to be nicer. My world is stable until Father arrives from the store one day with a supper announcement.

"I talked with Mr. Lehman at the store. He told me Peter is fighting in the war. Apparently, he completed six weeks of bootcamp in North Carolina and was deployed to England less than a month ago. A major battle is going to occur according to rumors. With this news, June, you may now go to the store to shop whenever you want. I no longer have to worry about you running into Peter."

"Great news, Father...the part about being able to shop again. The news about Peter is not good. I hope he stays safe and is not in danger."

"We all hope the same for him, June. Our Faith does not support war. We prefer peaceful resolutions to troubled times among countries. I will not allow you to follow what is happening in the war, ignore it. Our prayers should focus on a quick end to the war."

"Understood. I know Peter is not the only man who is overseas fighting for our country. I have heard of other young men from the community."

"Yes, there are several. We can pray for them, but we need to remain distant from the war itself. We cannot support it."

"I do hope differences are resolved for all involved. It is frightening to think young men are risking their lives for our freedom."

"Agreed. Now, what's for dessert Rebekah?"

At supper's end, I ask to be relieved to read the Bible. I try to do so, but my thoughts keep drifting back to Peter's touch and gentleness. He is alive in my heart and soul. He has to be safe; I need him to return to rescue me. He slipped a picture of himself into my shawl in the hay mow. He knew I could not accept it as it is an image of him; pictures are vanity at its worst. There is no way I can burn or toss it; I want to see Peter as often as I can sneak a peek. I wish I could have given him one of me; but alas, having a picture taken is forbidden. I hope he remembers me as often as I recall him. I love him so much. The world is a happier place for me with the memory of our time together being a vivid component of my days. I know he will return, and we will be together. Please war, end soon.

Chapter 46
First Signs—April 7, 1944
(Good Friday)

The flower bulbs we planted in the garden are bearing buds of all the colors of the rainbow. The trees are bursting with their abundant spring green sprigs. The rabbits and squirrels run rampant throughout the yard and fields. The cacophony of different bird sounds causes me to smile. The birds' harmonious chirping reflects my constant state of glee. What a difference time has given me. I am in love!

As we gather for supper, I begin to feel sick. Mother notices and asks if I am okay. I reply it must have been something I ate last night. I excuse myself, rush upstairs, and vomit. Food poisoning? No one else is sick though. Must be a bug I caught at the meetinghouse or school. I clean myself and return to eat and help with clearing the table.

As I finish Bible study for the evening, I am exhausted even though it is only 8:30 p.m. How can I be this fatigued as today's chores were not strenuous. I take a sponge bath in preparation for an early night's rest. As I clean my left breast, I feel a tenderness I have never felt before. It hurts to the touch. I sponge my right breast with a resulting similar sensation. My monthlies are probably starting soon. My nightgown is heavy against my breasts as I slide into bed. I am exhausted and fall asleep quickly.

As the days go by, more signs of spring appear. The hours of sunshine are getting longer. Temperatures are still cool in the mornings and evenings but are pleasant in the afternoons. I think of Peter daily and wish I could learn how he is doing. Perhaps I can ask Mr. Lehman if he has heard from him. I will need to work it into a conversation somehow in order not to appear too forward. Maybe Mother needs some ingredients for the dishes for the Good Friday potluck supper at the meetinghouse.

"Mother, have you decided what we will take to the Good Friday potluck supper?"

"No, I have not even begun to think about this but need to soon. Do you have any suggestions?"

"How about sweet potato and shoo fly pies and a platter of pickled eggs? We have sweet potatoes and red beets still in the icehouse."

"Those are great ideas June. I will need to get a few ingredients to make them."

"Let me go to the store for you. When you know what you need, I will see if I can get a ride to town with Father."

"Did I hear my name mentioned?" Father asks.

"Why yes, John, you did. Would you take June to town so she can get what we need to make food for the upcoming Good Friday supper?"

"Sure, I am going to the feed mill tomorrow. Is tomorrow soon enough?"

"Works for me Father. Thank you!" The scheme is working perfectly so far! I hope to hear about Peter tomorrow; I pray he is okay.

— ∞ —

"Hi Mr. Lehman," I say as I enter the store.

"Why June, so nice to see you. It seems like it's been a long time since you were in the store. How are the family and the farm?"

"Everyone and everything is fine. Spring is showing itself everywhere I turn. I love the rebirth of the trees, the budding of the flowers, and the smell of fresh cut grass. We have a few new calves too. How are you doing?"

"Working way too hard these days with Peter gone."

A perfect segue for me to ask if he has heard from him.

"You have not hired anyone to help you with the store?"

"No, I decided to wait to see if Peter returns from the war. He is a good assistant; I don't want to take the time to train another person if Peter can return soon."

"Do you think he will return soon; have you heard from him? He has been gone several months, right?" I try to act nonchalant, as if I have not counted the days and hours since he left.

"He sent me a short V-mail letter a couple of weeks ago saying he was settling in over there in England. No mention of how pretty he finds the English women though. He's participating in daily drills to prepare for his role in the war. He's hoping the war will end soon, so he doesn't have to fight. The letter was short as they tend to be with V-mail and sentences were blacked out."

"Glad he wrote you to give you an update. It would be good if he did not have to go to battle. Preparing for war is one thing; being in one is a different story. Our Faith does not believe in war, but we love our country and want it to remain."

"Men like Peter who believe it is their duty to serve our country, make us proud. They are protecting us from Hitler coming to the United States. We must stop his progression before he gets too powerful."

"I understand. Well, enough about Peter. Here is the list of items Mother needs this trip."

"This is a short list, and luckily, I have everything. It will take me a few minutes to gather and package the items for you. Why don't you have a root beer on me while you wait. There are bottles deep in the icebox."

"I am thirsty. Thank you, Mr. Lehman." He does not realize how thankful I am for the shared information.

Chapter 47
Divulgence—April 1944

"Thank you for getting the ingredients I needed from the store, June. Do you want to help me with making the pies and eggs?" Mother asks.

"Happy to. What would you like me to do?"

"Would you peel the red beets and the sweet potatoes? I will work on the pastry for the pie crusts."

I gather the vegetables from the root cellar and wash them carefully, as they had been stored all winter long. I peel the potatoes and dice them so they will cook faster and be able to be mashed for the pie filling. The red beets are a little tougher to peel due to their extensive roots. I find the color of the water a little nauseating. I start to swoon and sit as I feel dizzy.

"Are you okay, June?" Mother inquires. "You look pale, and I see you are sweating, yet it is cool in the kitchen."

I cannot respond as I feel terrible and need to get some air. I make it to the herb garden before dinner hits the ground. I wipe my mouth with a hankie and stand still for a few moments. Mother is soon beside me taking my arm to lead me back into the kitchen. I sit at the table.

Mother gives me an intense look, and asks me a difficult question, one I think she intuitively knows the answer. "June, have you had your monthlies recently?"

Shocked, I think back and realize I have not. "Come to think of it, Mother, I believe the last time was in February. Why?"

"Well, between missing your monthlies and the recent nauseous spells, I would say you are with child, but that is impossible, is it not?"

I peer into her eyes and admit timidly it is possible. I burst into tears. Mother holds me until I reach a break in the flow.

"I was afraid you and Peter might have been together. You are more confident and reassured. You are walking lighter and seem much happier. I should have known."

"Mother, it was the most glorious thing to ever happen to me. Before Peter left for Europe, he stopped by to tell me he was departing the next day. One thing led to another, and it was impossible to resist each other, not knowing if he would be safe and ever return. We pledged our love to one another and united. It was the most wonderful evening of my life. He promised to return and marry me. I assured him I would wait for him and look forward to our life together. He has to return,

Mother. And if I am with child, he has even more reason to come back to me. I love him so much and hope you understand. I know it was not what I should have done according to the Faith; but I am human, and these are extenuating circumstances. We are meant for each other, and apparently God feels the same way to bless our union with a child. I need to let Peter know somehow."

"June, we need to think about this carefully and decide what is best for your future. Being an unwed mother in our Faith is a sin. While you believe you are in love, you have limited experience and now have harmed a future for any marriage prospect within the Faith. Father is going to be extremely upset. I need to tell him soon though, as you will be showing soon. While I appreciate your feelings for Peter and am not surprised, as I could see you were infatuated with him, I do not think Father will understand at all. I will approach him with the news but ask you not to share this with anyone. We need to find out if you are indeed with child. I will arrange for a midwife to come when the rest of the family is away, so as not to arouse suspicion. Perhaps it is a false alarm."

I am taken back. This is all too much. I am overjoyed I might be carrying Peter's child. I want others to be as happy as I am, but I am sure Father will be quite embarrassed and will not be pleased. I need to keep Mother on my side, so she can persuade him to let me have the baby.

"Okay Mother. I think having a midwife visit would be good. No sense being overly concerned if I am not pregnant. Please arrange a day. We can go from there with other plans as warranted. Thank you, and I trust you know I mean no harm to anyone."

Chapter 48

Regrets—June 3, 1944

New York City

Well, now you may have a clue why I am in New York City. It is not because I am here for fun. I am with child; the midwife confirmed it. She assured me it is not a false alarm, and I am probably a couple of months along. Mother shared the news with Father. She supported me and tried to get Father to let me have the child and raise it with the hope Peter would keep his promise and wed me when he returns. But I will let them tell the story of what happened between them. I only have two free nights in town and want to make the most of them.

I had planned on retiring after supper to prepare for tomorrow. However, it dawns on me, I could go out on the town. After all, this is New York City—the city that never sleeps. I am tense thinking of tomorrow; maybe a little walk around town would help to settle me, and I would get to see some famous sights.

As I leave the lobby, the concierge sees me and calls me over to her station. "I see the city has captured your spirit and you are feeling adventurous—no?"

"Why yes, I enjoyed the most delicious supper at Gusto's—thank you for the recommendation. I thought I would take a walk outside. I assume it is okay to walk alone around the hotel?"

"Yes, it is fine. This area is safe but always keep an eye out for strange activities or people. I recommend a walk—here's some sights to see along the way. Check in when you return, so I know you are okay."

"I will. Thank you so much for all the help and for caring. It means a lot to me."

As I exit the hotel, the smell of the city hits me, as does its vibrance. There are so many people walking about. It is a beautiful spring night, and the city is aglow with lights of different shapes and rainbow colors. I walk along 45th Street. The stores are still open. A shoe store catches my eye. Now is the chance to try on heels. A young female clerk meets me at the door.

"Good evening. Welcome to our store. My name is Emily, and I'm here to assist you. Is there a particular shoe style of interest?"

"You can see, my shoes are very basic. I'd like to try on a pair of heels for the first time."

"Any particular color?"

"How about red?"

"You're in luck. We have several pairs in red, and some are on sale. What size do you wear?"

"That's a great question. I'm not sure. The shoes I'm wearing are sevens."

"Why don't I measure your feet to be sure?"

"Is there a cost for that?"

"Oh no, we do it for free using this contraption. If you want to remove your shoes, I'll measure both feet to be sure of your size."

I sit down and untie my homely shoes. They are so ugly and basic.

"Here we are—two lovely pairs to try."

The clerk is very patient with me as I try on two different pairs. She gives me short nylons to put on before I place the shoes on my feet. Both pairs feel very tight and uncomfortable. How do women walk in such things?

"I'm afraid I'm going to have to say no to them. They hurt my feet, and I have nowhere to wear them."

"That's a shame, as they look wonderful on you."

"Thank you so much for your time. I really appreciate it."
I exit as fast as I can. I will never be a fashion statement.
Continuing down the street, I see a children's store. The store
has a huge section of toys, nursery furniture, and clothes
arranged by age groups. Heading to the newborn area, I see
racks of clothes for boys and girls plus cute displays. I wonder
what I will have. The pink dresses catch my eye and touching
them, I muse about what kind of mother I will be. Fair, strict,
kind, fun, protective or—and then it dawns on me I will not be
a mother for much longer. How cruel can life be?

Flustered, tears pour down my cheeks and I stop mid step.
I think of my parents. A sudden urge comes over me to write a
letter to them to tell them I made it safely to New York City. I
know they love me and think they have done the right thing for
me and our family. I did not leave happily, and now I am sad I
was not more understanding of how hard it is to be a parent.
They did not ask me to love Peter; in fact, they discouraged me
from courting a man not of our Faith. I violated an unwritten
agreement by getting pregnant and now am forcing them to
rectify the situation. They are doing the best they can.
Parenting is not easy. I need to let them know I appreciate their
involvement, even though I wish the outcome could be

different. I want to have Peter's child, as I know he will return to me. He loves me and I love him.

Rushing back to the hotel, I inform the concierge of my return and ask if she has any stationery. She tells me there is some in the desk in my room. The stationery is in a packet in the desk drawer. A sheet falls out, which I pick up off the floor, and I try to write to my parents. This is more difficult than I imagined. I am still so angry. I want this child and yet, I realize that I cannot provide for it. I do not have a job, any income, a place to live if I get shunned, and no support system to help me if my family must disown me. I have no choice but to have an abortion. I will rest and rise early tomorrow to write them after breakfast.

I write to Peter instead to tell him about the baby. I will have to trust my parents will give him my letter if something happens to me, as I have no other way to deliver it. I will put the finished letter in my bag with his name on the envelope. This letter is difficult to draft. How can I express my feelings and share my desire to have his baby in a way without making my parents sound evil? I wish Peter was here with me. He would be supportive and caring and would promise to marry me and take care of our child. It is unfair he does not have a say in the future of the child we have created.

New York City

June 3, 1944

My Dear Peter,

Would you believe I am writing to you from New York City? It's quite a place from what little I have seen. City life is exciting as tons of people are bustling about and there are so many stores and restaurants. A train brought me here from Philadelphia. A driver met me at the train station and transported me to the hotel. It's been a little intimidating to say the least, but tonight I enjoyed an Italian supper at a restaurant near my hotel. I've used an elevator to get to my room. I even tried on heels at a shoe store for the first time. It's amazing women can walk in them all day. They are so uncomfortable.

Why am I in New York City? It's a long story. If only you were here with me, I could tell you all of this in person. If you were here though, I probably wouldn't be here. We would be together and so happy. But, that's not to be.

There's no easy way to say this, so I'm just going to come out and tell you why I'm here. We conceived a child Peter, in the hay mow. You can imagine my surprise and the reaction of my parents when they discovered we had sex out of wedlock and my pregnancy. My parents explored options, and Father decided I should get an abortion. It would save the family's pride and place within the Faith. I tried to change his mind, but couldn't, and since I'm not yet 18, I must abide by his wishes. He identified a doctor who will perform the procedure. I want us to be together and raise our child, but it's not to be.

So tomorrow I will learn about the procedure and have the abortion the next day. After two more nights in New York City, I will return home. No one else knows about this except my parents, a midwife, and now you. Sharing any information about the procedure places the doctor at risk as well as our family. Since you are the father, I thought it proper you know. To me it is a sign from God he wants us to be together. He blessed us with a creation from our love. We'll never know what we would have had—a girl or a boy—but hopefully, we can have others once you return from the war. I know you will come back to me, and we will get married and raise a wonderful family of our own.

This news is jolting, I'm sure. I wanted you to hear it from me though. You need to protect yourself and be sure to return home safely. I love you even more than I thought possible and will do whatever it takes to be with you forever, my love. You have my word.

Wish I could kiss you and embrace you with the deep intensity of my feelings. There will be time for that in the future. Be safe my darling until we meet again.

Lovingly,

June

Chapter 49
The Confrontation—May 1944
Reading, Pennsylvania

"John, I need to talk to you in private. Will you join me in the potting shed soon?"

"Sure Rebekah, let me finish feeding the horses and I will soon be there."

"John, please close the door and join me on the bench. I hope you have time to talk, as we need to do so. I have been suspecting June has fallen for Peter—her behavior changes when she is near him and she has told me she thinks she loves him."

"I also think she is falling for him and not Michael Wenger. I have tried to encourage her to think about the consequences of courting someone not of the Faith. Why are you mentioning this though. Peter is not here now; perhaps there is a chance for us to have June see Michael more while Peter is away."

"I do not know how to tell you this, but the horse is out of the barn, as the saying goes."

"Yuh? I am lost Rebekah."

"It is too late to keep June and Peter apart. She is carrying his child." Total silence ensues. "John, hello, you are scaring me with your silence."

"I need to say a prayer first to regain composure. I need guidance on how to respond. Without such, my initial reaction is I cannot believe our daughter has put us in this predicament. She has always been a good child and now to embarrass us in front of our fellow meetinghouse members and the community by being an unwed mother…carrying a child of an English man—one not of our Faith…there is no forgiving this. I need time to absorb this information and to prepare a proper reaction. I need to seek guidance, as I surely cannot go to the bishop or to our minister, Mr. Wenger, since he is Michael's father. They would be appalled and would have to excommunicate June from the Faith for a while."

"Take the time you need, but I hope we can discuss this. Our daughter has been a great child and is growing into a beautiful woman. She made a mistake, but she is young, and the situation is unusual. We need to carefully go ahead with any plans to protect her as well as the rest of our family. I have ideas, so once you are ready to discuss, please let me know."

A week passes before John is ready to further discuss June's condition. He calls Rebekah into the barn after supper.

"I have given our situation much thought and have gotten some advice. I decided to speak with a doctor, a referral by the midwife. I explained our situation and told him about the parameters of our Faith, and its beliefs concerning having children out of wedlock to an English father. He listened carefully and provided me with several options. The first option would be to let June have the child. He did not realize it, but this would mean she would have to leave the Faith at least temporarily, and we would have to shun her and have no contact with her or the baby. The second option would be to let her carry the child and have it be adopted. This would require her to go away during her pregnancy, so others would not be aware of her condition. It would also mean she would never get to be a part of the baby's life. The third option is for her to have an abortion. She is still early enough in her pregnancy for this to be possible. It is illegal though, and she would have to go to a physician who is willing to perform such a procedure. He knows of a doctor in New York City and gave me his contact information. The fourth would be to pray for a miscarriage, but she is healthy and unlikely to have one. These are our four options, no easy choice."

"I see you have given this deep thought, and I thank you for consulting with a physician. I know what I prefer to do, but I would like to hear your choice first before I voice mine."

"I think there is only one option, personally. We do not have any guarantee Peter will return from the war, and even if he does, he may be injured and not be able to provide for a family. June cannot care for herself and a child without our or Peter's help. She is healthy and praying for a miscarriage seems cruel and wrong. We only have one option—an abortion. Killing a fetus is wrong, I am aware, but it would preserve the pride our family has had over generations in the Faith. It would be a one-time cost versus having to provide for a child for life. It would give June another chance to begin a new life—still in the Faith, as no one would be aware what has transpired. Peter would not be told. She may end up with him, or she may marry someone else. She can have other children. I see this as our only choice."

"I am respectful of your wisdom and position, husband. I am sad to hear this is your preference. I think we owe June more than this. She will be scared to go to New York City, a big city, let alone frightened of the abortion itself. I do not know what an abortion entails and would like to know more details before we force her to have one. I think we might want to leave the Faith if it means leaving behind our beloved daughter and her child. What kind of religion requires such? It is inhumane. My preference would be option one—for her to have the baby, and we help raise it if Peter is out of the picture.

I can tell June loves him; it will break her to force her to get rid of a part of him within her. I know this will be a big change for all of us, as we will need to find a new religion where unwed mothers are welcome. There must be a religion permitting this. She is our child and is having our first grandchild. Otherwise, we are murdering a fetus which is so very wrong."

"Rebekah, I have heard your druthers, but you know, I am the head of this family and what I decide stands. This is not an easy decision. I will talk with the doctor again to understand what is involved with an abortion. I will continue to pray, as I suggest you do. We need guidance with making this decision. There is no ideal option."

"Yes, John. I understand. For now, I will not share any details with anyone other than you and June. I pray we can make the best decision for all involved."

Chapter 50
Anticipation—May 1944

"Mother, have you told Father about me being with child?"

'Yes, June, I did."

"And?"

"As you can imagine, he is not pleased. He loves you, but he feels threatened by this situation. He is a man of strong faith, and a child out of wedlock bears strict consequences for him and our family. He has talked with a physician to understand options and is going to gather more details so we can make an informed decision. I say we, but you know, it ultimately is Father's decision, as he is the head of this household and you are underage."

"I understand, Mother, and I do not mean to be disrespectful, but it is my life, Peter's and my child's. I feel I should have some say in the decision, as it affects me the most."

"I know it does June, but you are aware of how the Faith works, and the hierarchy followers need to abide by to remain in the Faith. Once we have all the options, the three of us will discuss them together. Meanwhile, it is best you do not talk about your pregnancy with anyone but Father and me. Okay?"

"Yes, Mother. Please do try and work with Father, though, as much as you can. I love Peter and know he will come back to me. We will become a family. I have thought about it, and I have accepted leaving the Faith to marry him and make our child a home. All will turn out okay. I have faith."

Chapter 51

Time Passage—May 1944

"June, when you are finished with clearing the dishes, Father and I would like to talk with you."

"Yes, Mother. I should be done in about 15 minutes. I hope this is about what I think it is. Time has passed and I need to know what you have been thinking."

"Yes, we need to discuss a lot of things. We will meet in the potting shed in about 20 minutes. I will let Father know."

"Thank you, Mother."

I cannot help but pace as I dry the supper dishes. It had been over a week since I last talked with Mother about the baby. I pray they have reached the right decision about what to do. Time will soon tell.

"This is the first time you and I have talked directly about your being with child from a man who is not of our Faith. I am disappointed in you. You have been a wonderful daughter and a good Christian. I had high hopes for you and envisioned you getting married soon. I did not foresee you engaging with an English man out of wedlock resulting in a pregnancy.

"Prayers and guidance have been issued and sought as to what to do. I want to be a loving father, but also a pillar of the community and a respected man of our religious sect. I believe Mother told you I talked with a physician outside of the area about our options. Considering them, as head of our household, there is only one practical option. I have begun making arrangements for you to travel to New York City, where a physician is willing to conduct an anonymous abortion. By anonymous, I mean, he will not inform our community and will keep the procedure as private as possible. He is taking a risk performing such a procedure, as it is illegal in the state. I know this comes as a great shock, but I hope you can see this is the only way for all of us to stay together. No one else within the Faith will know.

"You will travel by train alone to the physician's office, where the procedure will take place. You need to go before an abortion becomes unsafe. I will pay for travel, accommodation, meals, and the procedure. Mother is not in agreement with this, as she wishes you would have and keep the baby. I cannot afford to lose you and will not allow the Faith to shun you for this wrong nor have shame transferred to our entire family. Your siblings and we, your parents, deserve better. We want to stay in the Faith and want you to stay there too. This is a difficult decision, one of the hardest I have ever had to make,

222

but it is a necessary plan to maintain our position in the Plain community."

My hands grab my heart and tears drip from my eyes. What is happening? I cannot decide my own future? I must be subjected to the wishes of Father, the patriarch of the family. He is right, it is his decision to make according to the rules of our house and Faith. I wish I could be anywhere but here. I do not want to respond to my parents; I want to run and escape reality.

"As Father says, June, I wish you could have the child and raise it here. I really do," Mother says. "But I must defer to Father. Your actions have caused this pregnancy, and it is not fair to the rest of us to suffer for what you have done. I need to consider each of my precious children. You will be able to have other babies once you are married, and then you will understand what a burden this decision is to all of us. We want the best for you and for everyone. An abortion is the best answer. You will need to keep this secret; otherwise, why terminate this pregnancy? You cannot tell your grandparents, aunts and uncles, siblings, cousins, other relatives, and friends. Understand?"

With extreme willpower I say, "I thank you for deciding. It is not to my liking, but I have no choice but to obey you both. I need to leave now; may I be excused?"

"You may," Father says. "Think it over and we will talk again. I will get an appointment with the physician and arrange for the train ticket and hotel room. Again, time is of the essence."

Chapter 52
Travel Arrangements—May 1944

Father has requested I meet him in the barn. Approaching the door, my feet move stiffly, and my heart is heavy.

"June, I want to share your arrangements. I made an appointment with a doctor for the beginning of June. You will meet with his nurse the day before the procedure to gather your vital statistics and to review the process. The doctor recommends you return home the day after the procedure. I have purchased a roundtrip train ticket from Philadelphia to New York City. I have booked a room for you at the Roosevelt Hotel for three nights. I will give you cash to pay for it, as well as to cover meals and incidentals. The doctor emphasized the need to be private about this. He could get into a lot of legal trouble if word leaks he is performing such procedures. He is doing us a favor, and we need to honor his wishes. This gives you a week to prepare. I will review the city with you, pointing out on a map where the train station is located and how to get to the hotel. I will do the same with how to get to the doctor's office. Any questions?"

"Appears you have thought of every detail, Father. I will process this and think about what to pack. I will appreciate the review of how to get around in the city, as you know it will be a first time for me. I admit, I am leery of what is going to happen. I assume the doctor will inform me how to prepare for the procedure and how to care for myself afterwards?"

"I have been assured he is the best doctor in the area to do an abortion, or I would not subject you to him. He comes highly recommended. He is a Columbia medical school graduate and has written several surgical books."

"He does sound like he knows what he is doing. I will have faith," I say tongue in cheek. Inside, I am so mad I am ready to hit a wall. It is my life and my baby. I resent how I am being treated and cannot believe my parents will murder a child. We do not believe in war, yet we will kill a baby? The irony. The double standard. My poor baby. Words escape me, but I cannot express them even if I did have them handy. Is this parental love? If only Peter could be here to help fight this decision and prove his love for me to my parents.

Chapter 53
Unrest—May 1944

"I do not feel right about what we did, John. June is our daughter, and a good one. She made a terrible error in judgement during a difficult emotional time. We are sending her away to get an abortion. Is this what God would want us to do? Is he so unforgiving? The poor child has gotten pregnant. She did not know how to prevent it, as I never talked to her about such measures. She trusted someone she feels she is in love with. How do we know he is not trustworthy? I feel awful about this."

"Rebekah, I appreciate your feelings and concern. As I have expressed, this is not an easy decision for me to make. There is no winning no matter what option we take. We have good standing in our Faith, our community, and so do the family members we raised. June has put all of this in jeopardy through her actions. She completely ignored our advice to not get involved with a man outside of our Faith. She went against our counsel and has to suffer the consequences. Having a child to care for at her age would be worse. She would be shunned and so would we. I do not feel I should have to leave my religion because of what she did. If she has the baby, she will be alone. There is no assurance Peter will return, and if by some lucky chance he survives the war, there is no guarantee he will stand by June and marry her. He may suffer emotionally from the war also. This would not make him a good partner for her or a good father or provider for the baby.

"Sending her away until she has the baby and letting someone adopt it is out of the question. The child could come back in time to find its real mother and cause an assortment of issues for us. Besides, this would be a constant emotional drain on June. She will always wonder what happened to the child and be sad she gave it away.

"There is no option but the one I proposed. We must go through with it," John says.

"John, what do you think the bishop would advise about the options. I know you do not want to consult with him, but maybe he has experience with this type of situation and would offer helpful advice. Is he compelled to keep our predicament confidential?"

"I am unsure what the bishop is obligated to do with such information. I think it would cause a real conflict for him. By telling him, we are burdening him with our lives, and he would need to do what is best for the majority. He cannot lie to the members. I strongly feel we should not confide in him."

"Is there anyone else you can talk to? Anyone who might have an insight into what else may be possible?"

"At this point, we do not have time to contemplate any other possibilities. June needs to have an abortion soon. She is in more danger as time passes. We need to act, my decision stands. She will go to New York City to have an abortion. We will deal with the aftermath and keep this secret from others. It will save her dignity, as well as ours."

Chapter 54

Preparation Day—June 4, 1944
New York City

A pigeon cooing near the hotel window wakes me. I rise and look at the massive view of the city. It is time for me to get a shower and get dressed to visit the doctor in preparation for the abortion tomorrow. My shoulders are heavy with the weight of the day. I am not in my body, but an observer, like a character in a play who is doing what she is directed to do. I get on my knees and pray to God asking again for his forgiveness and for the strength to do what I must to fulfill my Father's wishes. I feel my stomach, and while I cannot feel any movement, I am aware of the baby within me. Today, it is a part of me, but as of tomorrow, it will no longer exist. Is this why they say life is precious? It is given so easily and can be taken away rapidly. I am a mother today, but not for long. I can only hope I will be able to conceive again when Peter and I get married. I know he will want children, and I want to be their mother. I pray for his safety so he can return to me.

I eat breakfast in the hotel restaurant. When the food arrives, the smell is repulsive, and I realize I am not hungry. I drink a little juice and eat some oatmeal. I look around; it seems like an ordinary day for many people. Most are businessmen reading newspapers. I see one other single woman and wonder about her story. What brings her to New York City and what will she do today? Shop? Attend a play? Visit with friends?

"Sweetie, you're going to get thin really quick if you don't eat more food," the kind server says.

I think to myself—I am going to get thin, but for another reason than not eating. I want to scream *I am having an abortion*, but of course, I do not. I make an excuse about having cramps; she empathizes with me.

"Drink more hot tea, it will help settle those nasty muscles."

I obey, as I am doing with my parents. The tea tastes good. I have a second cup. My bill arrives and I pay with the cash Father gave me. There still is money in my bag, but most of it will go to the doctor. My Father wants me to pay him in cash, so there will be no record. He wants to prevent anyone from ever finding out about the procedure. It is the best for all, he says. I keep repeating those words *Best for All* as I leave the restaurant. Maybe if I say it enough, I will start to believe it.

Once in my room, I write to my parents.

New York City

June 4, 1944

Dear Mother & Father,

I will try and write you a few lines this morning to let you know that I am well. I can sleep well and can eat well. My good appetite has not left me yet. I get oatmeal and plenty of other things for breakfast and strawberries and new sliced tomatoes with other things for supper. Everything is very good.

Well, I cannot say that I have had home sickness yet. I felt a little nervous and excited at first, everything being so strange, but it seems I am getting used to the surroundings. I have learned some of Paul's writings, where he says I have learned in what state and condition I am in, there with to be contented.

I took a walk yesterday eve on the street, one square to a park, you might think I am raking through town. The park was a very pretty place, but I cared little, for it seems it was the air and exercise I wanted. Well, I hardly know what more to write but would ask you to remember me in your prayers. I almost feel sometimes as though I was driven away from all I have in this world, but again I feel that the Lord is my shepherd—I shall not want.

I hope when these few lines come to hand, they will find you enjoying good health.

I will close for this time by sending you and all my best wishes...

Your Unworthy Daughter

June

As I leave, I hand my parent's letter to the hotel desk clerk for it to be mailed. I confirm how to get to the address I was given for the doctor's office. It is only a block away, and it does not take me long to get there. The office is on the second floor. I take the stairs, see the hall sign pointing to the right, and enter a small waiting area. There is no desk clerk to greet me or other patients. The air is sterile and reeks of antiseptic. Soon, a woman in a nurse's uniform appears and asks if I am June Davis.

"Yes, I am June."

"I'm Miss Paxon, a nurse. I take it you found us easily, as you are right on time. Please follow me."

We walk down a long hall to an exam room.

"You may hang your shawl and bag on the hook. I need to weigh you; the less things hanging on you, the better."

Miss Paxon weighs me, takes my blood pressure, and temperature. She checks my pulse.

"Your health seems fine. Do you have any known drug allergies or health conditions?"

"Nothing I am aware of. I have been healthy and have not been to many doctors. We tend to have healers in our community who help when we are ill."

"Tell me about the community in which you live."

"It is a rural one in Pennsylvania. I am of the Plain Faith, meaning we put our health in God's hands. We do not believe in medicines, but more in natural remedies."

"Interesting. Does being Plain mean a lot to you?"

"I thought it did. I do not know any other life, as I was raised in a community of Plain people. This pregnancy is outside of our norm. That is why I am here. My community shuns unwed mothers. Father has decided I should have this abortion. It will save face with the meetinghouse membership and will allow me to avoid excommunication."

"How do you feel?"

"Frankly, no one has asked me, but you. One thing about our Faith—we are taught to be obedient. As a woman under 18, Father is responsible for me, and I must abide by his wishes."

"Would you do things differently if you were free to make the decision?"

I am not sure why the nurse is being so caring, but I converse with her as she seems harmless. She is a woman and has experience with pregnancies apparently. This is an opportunity to say what I feel, and I take it.

"You are the only person to ask me this question. If it were left to me, I would have the child, as I know its father will return from the war and marry me and provide a great home for us."

"So, the father is in the war? Is he overseas?"

"Yes, he joined the army because Father forbade him to court me. He thought there was no reason to stay due to Father's mandate and his sense of obligation to serve in the war. He could have gotten deferred, as he used to assist his father with butchering animals and caring for them beforehand. He came home between bootcamp and being sent to Europe. He told me he loved me and would return to me; he wanted me to wait for him. I promised I would. One thing led to another, and here I am. An unwed mother of Plain Faith who is ending her pregnancy."

"You have been though a lot. I feel for you and know this can't be easy. We will try and make it as easy as possible. I want to talk about what an abortion entails. We will do what is called a D&C procedure. That's shorthand for dilation and curettage.

235

The doctor will expand your cervix, the entry channel to your uterus, using a tool called a curettage to scrape the sides of the uterus. This will detach the fertilized egg implanted in the uterine wall. The removed egg ends the pregnancy. From the puzzled look, do you know where the cervix and uterus are located?"

"I know they are inside of me, but not much more," I reply.

"Let me show you. Here's an illustration of a woman's internal reproductive organs. This is the uterus. It holds a baby. The cervix is the opening to the uterus and is located here. The uterus gets a temporary attachment, called a placenta, with a cord attached to the baby. Through it air and nutrients are provided to the baby and waste is removed. Does this all make sense?"

"I think so. Will I be awake while this is happening?"

"You will be given sodium pentothal. It will make you drowsy; you will fall asleep until the procedure is over."

"Is it painful?"

"Some women experience pain, some don't. It is hard to predict. There are possible complications I need to tell you about though. These include infections, tears in the uterus, and excessive bleeding afterwards.

"We will monitor your vital signs. An abortion currently is illegal in this state, so we ask you to maintain confidentiality. We will do the same. No mention of why you are a patient of ours will ever be given to anyone. The doctor could get into a lot of trouble if others learn he performs this procedure. In time, we hope this will change, so abortions will be available to those who need or want them. The laws are behind human behavior once again. Sex is a common thing; one should not have to hide resulting pregnancies. It happens to more women than you may think. The doctor here sides with women and wants the best for them."

"This is a lot of information, and most of it is new to me. I did not know what an abortion meant except it would remove a baby. I am scared. I hope you will tell my parents if anything goes wrong. I am here in New York City by myself. You will need to write them as they do not own a telephone. They do not want anyone to know about this, so confidentiality is key. How long will this take?"

"We will start the procedure tomorrow morning with me prepping you; I would allow two to three hours for this. We want you to stay after the procedure to be sure there are no complications. I would allow at least five hours total. We will place pads in your panties for any post external bleeding and give you extras. Will you be staying in the city tomorrow night? We recommend it."

"Yes, I have a hotel room for two more nights. What do I need to do tonight to prepare?"

"Absolutely nothing. I would try not to think too much about the abortion process. You will be in good hands. Again, the doctor cares about women like you who are in tough situations. He is extraordinary and trained at a great medical school here in our state. I would go to him if I needed an abortion."

"That is comforting. Oh, when do I pay you? I want to pay in cash and have it with me."

"Let's take care of the payment since you have the cash. I apologize for the amount, but we need to cover expenses and risks. Do you have the exact amount?"

"Yes, here it is. Please count the money."

As she was counting, I recall the intimate night with Peter and how I would do it all again knowing the outcome. I love him so much and feel his presence with me now. I am sorry

Peter; I hope you can forgive me. Give me courage and strength.

"The amount is correct. I won't issue a receipt as no record is desired by either party. If there's no other questions, I'll see you here at 9 a.m. tomorrow morning. The doctor will spend some time talking with you prior to the procedure. Wear a dress and panties. Otherwise, have as good of a night as you can. We will see you tomorrow."

"Thank you. I will be here at 9 a.m."

Chapter 55
Another Viewpoint—June 4, 1944
Peter—Somewhere in England

England is very different than rural Pennsylvania. I have been stationed here in preparation for a major operation. General Eisenhower has informed us what we are about to do will change history. In fact, yesterday, he issued this message:

Soldiers, Sailors, and Airmen of the Allied Expeditionary Force!

You are about to embark upon the Great Crusade, toward which we have striven these many months. The eyes of the world are upon you. The hope and prayers of liberty-loving people everywhere march with you. In company with our brave Allies and brothers-in-arms on other Fronts, you will bring about the destruction of the German war machine, the elimination of Nazi tyranny over the oppressed peoples of Europe, and security for ourselves in a free world.

Your task will not be an easy one. Your enemy is well trained, well equipped and battle-hardened. He will fight savagely.

But this is the year 1944! Much has happened since the Nazi triumphs of 1940-41. The United Nations have inflicted upon the Germans great defeats, in open battle, man-to-man. Our air offensive has seriously reduced their strength in the air and their capacity to wage war on the ground. Our Home Fronts have given us an overwhelming superiority in weapons and munitions of war, and placed at our disposal great reserves of trained fighting men. The tide has turned! The free men of the world are marching together to Victory!

I have full confidence in your courage, devotion to duty and skill in battle. We will accept nothing less than full Victory!

Good luck! And let us beseech the blessing of Almighty God upon this great and noble undertaking.

When a general takes the time to write, you know it can't be good. I fear for what lies ahead. I have been practicing with my fellow soldiers on artillery maneuvers, but how much practice is enough? Apparently, we have had all we are going to get. Tomorrow, bright and early, we will approach the target in what is being called Operation Overlord. This meek Pennsylvania man is going to be a key part of the action, as I will be in the first group to meet the enemy.

When I joined the war, I felt I had to. Our country needs to retain its freedom, and I wanted to help protect this privilege. Am I happy with my decision now? In theory, yes. It was the right thing to do—to enlist. I felt I wouldn't be permitted to share my life with June. However, since I joined the army, I have fallen deeply in love with this beautiful woman—inside and out—and that changes so much. I have matured and understand how deep my feelings are for her. I need to let her know. I will send a letter to Mr. Lehman for him to give to June when she comes into the store. It is the only way I can reach her; I feel strongly I need to reassure her of my abiding love.

Thinking of the V-mail process, I write:

Mr. Lehman—please give this letter to June Davis for me. Miss you and trust all is well. Peter

— ∞ —

June 4, 1944

Dearest June,

I miss you more than you will ever know. You captured my heart; I think about you constantly. I wish I could talk with you, but it is not possible. There is so much I wish I could share about how I have grown by being part of the army, and how much I have come to realize I need you in my life to be complete. The thought of you is what keeps me going. How I wish I could have received letters from you like so many of my army buddies have from their wives and girlfriends. I have lived vicariously through the words they shared of news from the home country. Our situation is fraught with issues, but I need to let you know I want and need you so badly. The one night we got to be together haunts my soul in

242

the most enchanting and endearing way. I can smell your hair and skin

over the many miles separating us. You are forever with me my love.

We are not allowed to talk about what is happening here, but I want

to assure you I am yours. When I return, we will marry; you will become

my cherished wife. I love you beyond words and eagerly await seeing your

kind smile once again. Please know I am with you in spirit. With this

letter, I commit myself to you and only you. You are my joy, my sunshine,

the reason I rise each day, and my raison d'etre (see I have learned some

French). Take care my precious chère.

Love,

Peter

Now I have another letter to write, one to my cousin who has been a steadfast correspondent and supporter through thick and thin. He also is in the army, but he lives in Washington, D.C. If I write to him, he will get it before the others, as he is part of the military. I write:

June 4, 1944

Hi Old Man,

How is the soldier? I hope you and the better half are just fine and I know you both are doing O.K. Boy I sure would like to drop in for a Sun. afternoon and eve with you. We sure would have a lot to talk about.

I got your letter last night. Boy I sure was glad to hear from you. The only thing it takes you so darn long to answer my letters. Boy if you don't do better, I will have to get your wife after you. I bet you lead some life—home for supper and all night and then you talk about being a soldier. Boy you don't know anything about the real Army life. I hope you never have to learn it either. I think I am seeing enough for both of us. You know it is about 5 mo. since I have seen any of you and boy if you think that isn't a long time just try it. But some of the boys have been overseas almost 2 years so why should I gripe.

I sure was surprised to hear about Aunt Carrie. I guess she just could not stand the trip. It sure will be funny at home with Aunt Jenny and Aunt Carrie and all those other people gone. But I guess the old have to die and the young may die.

Listen son I am going to try and tell you something I hope you get what I mean and don't think I am trying to preach, but those guys that are coming back from overseas, they probably have been in some tight spots, and have heard the bullets singing, and Son you change some after a while. So don't think too bad of them for they probably are pretty good guys, only they have a chip on their shoulder around you fellows that have never been in it.

You said something about transferring into the Em [enlisted military]. Well son, it just isn't done here. I guess I would like it all right, but you seem to think it would be tougher than the Infantry 93rd. You are mistaken there, I know they have all branches of work where we only have one. But our one is really a tough one.

Well Sarg., I guess I will close and go to town and take in a movie. The pubs don't open till 1900 hrs and then the Scotch is so damn scarce you hardly ever get more than three or 4 shots. It is funny the English people use a pub like an old country store back home. They spend a whole evening sipping a pint or 2 of beer. They think it is funny the way we drink all in a hurry to get more. Well Butch be good to yourself and the Wife. Don't let her get you on K.P. too often.

Your Kid Cuz

Peter

P.S.: I hope you can make this all out.

P.S.S.: You said something about us having to take over the business around home pretty soon. I often wonder if we will be able to settle down to a life like we used to know. I suppose you will be thinking about the construction business, and I guess it is about as good as there is. There is going to be a lot of rebuilding to do after this is over. It scares the shit out of me what I even want to do if I get back. I guess I will marry a rich widow and retire. Ha Ha.

Chapter 56
Day Breaks—June 5, 1944
New York City

The sun is shining when I wake, and the day I have dreaded is beginning. I know what I must do, but forgive me Peter and our baby, for I know I am sinning. I pray to whatever God is out there to protect me as I abort our precious child. I realize it is only beginning to grow, but I wish it could continue its journey within me. No mother should be forced into this against her will. Why would God want this to happen? Pray for me, Father, for I have sinned. I must suffer the consequences, whatever the price.

I take a quick shower and dress. Eating right now is out of the question, so I skip breakfast and head to the doctor's office.

"Good morning, June," says Miss Paxon. "How are you doing this morning?"

"As good as can be expected," I quietly reply.

"I understand how difficult this is for you. Would you want me to let your parents know how you are doing? I can send a telegram, and of course, I won't mention the abortion."

"Kind of you. Here is the store information where the telegram should be sent."

"I'm glad to do this. Let's get your blood pressure and check on your vitals one more time before the doctor sees you."

"Hello Miss Davis, I'm Dr. Adams. I will be performing the abortion. I understand the nurse has explained the procedure to you and you still wish to continue. True?"

"I guess so."

"Okay, the nurse will give you a gown to wear, and I'll meet you in the adjoining room."

"Thank you, Dr. Adams."

"Put this gown on with the opening ties in the front," the nurse says. "You can use the restroom to change and then hang your clothes on the wall hook. I will put your duffel bag and valuables in a safe. You will be put under anesthesia as we discussed, but I'll be with you when you recover. Let me know when you are ready."

Within minutes, I am ready as I am eager to get this over with. The nurse and I enter the room where the doctor (I am sure his name is not Adams) is waiting. There is a prepared gurney with sterile coverings and metal hoops on each side of the one end, and a tray with an assortment of instruments lying on it.

"Please lie down June and put your feet in the stirrups. Miss Paxon, please guide her. I will put this mask over your head to administer the anesthesia. By the time I count to 10, if you can hear me, raise your hand. This will be over before you know it. One, two, three…"

The next thing I know, I am awake lying on a bed. The nurse sees me rouse and comes over.

"You did great; the procedure went extremely well. You need to rest for several hours so we can continue to check your vitals and be sure you have no post reaction to the anesthesia. I have written the promised parental telegram and will send it soon. This is what I said:

June 5, 1944

Mr. & Mrs. Davis:

The operation was performed upon your daughter and the Doctor asked me to write and tell you that she is doing "exceedingly well."

We will take good care of her so don't worry.

It sounds like a blur but when the nurse finishes, I tell her it sounds fine and thank her again for writing it. I am too weak emotionally to write to my parents at this moment. I still harbor much resentment at having to get rid of my baby.

My blood pressure is checked again, and the nurse gives me instructions on how to care for myself during the coming weeks. She asks if I am okay and I reply yes. I dress, pack the supplies offered, and stroll defeatedly back to the hotel. I ask the concierge if there is a way to get food delivered. She explains room service, shares a menu, and offers to place the order I select.

Once I get to my room, I place my feet on an ottoman. I am tired and hungry because I skipped breakfast and dinner, but I am more mentally fatigued than anything. I check the time; it is around 3 p.m. Tears start to flow. It is over; no more baby. No more physical connection with Peter. Father has made sure I do not have a reason to be with Peter in the future. I know deep inside I will be though; Peter will be a part of my life forever. His love got me through this, as the parental love I depended on to this point took a back seat. I mentally have swapped one man for another. Peter is now my man. I hope someday I will be able to forgive Father, but not yet. I drift off; a knock on the door revives me.

"Room service."

I accept the meal, sign for the charge, and eat like a lion. Food never tasted so good; I am famished. Upon finishing, I run to the restroom and vomit what I ate. I should have chewed slower. After putting on a nightgown, I crawl into bed. A good night's rest is needed. Things will look brighter tomorrow. I will pack in the morning before the afternoon train home.

Peter here. We are told to get a good night's rest as we will depart early tomorrow morning. It's 8 p.m., and I'm in my birthday suit, lying in bed, trying not to think of what tomorrow will bring. Good night, June, my love. You are my North Star always.

Book III

Chapter 57
D (&C) Day—June 6, 1944

Tossing and turning, I see Peter in the distance.

"Peter, is that you?"

He seems to hear me and turns to look at me, but his face is all bloody and his leg is blown off. The remaining stump is dripping blood. Peter appears gaunt and pale.

"Peter. It's me, June."

He continues to stare at me without saying a word. He cannot speak as he has no mouth. His face is completely gone. I scream causing me to wake up. I look around and realize where I am; I am in a hotel room. I slowly recall why I am here and look down at my body. There is blood pooled around my bottom, and I am hot—sweating profusely. The sheets are soaking wet. I try to rise, but I am not able. An invisible weight is holding my legs to the mattress. I struggle to retain consciousness but quickly slip back into a dream state.

— ∞ —

"June, I need you to help me. I've been hit, and I can't move. I see you in the distance, or at least, I think it's you. Why aren't you coming to my aid? I need help. I see how beautiful you are and can't wait for you to

hold me. Please come to me quickly, as I'm about to pass out. Please June, come to me!"

— ∞ —

Bright light shining in the window brings me back to reality. I glance around. This time I know exactly where I am. I am lying in even more blood, and I am burning up with my stomach feeling weird—a cramp-like feeling, but stronger and higher. It is like nothing I have ever felt before. I should rise, but I cannot move. I drift off once again.

— ∞ —

"Peter, please come over here and hold me. I need to tell you what has happened. We have a child; I mean, we had a child. I never got to see it since Father made me get rid of it. I did this today. It was horrible. I thought the pain would be intense, but the pain was more emotional than physical. I kept thinking I was getting rid of you. I need you. I love you. I am so sorry! Please forgive me."

— ∞ —

"June why aren't you coming over to me. It seems you are embarrassed. Don't you know I love you beyond words. I see your beautiful face and I want to hold you. Come over here please; don't be afraid. What has happened to me doesn't prevent us from loving one another. Why won't you come and join me?"

— ∞ —

A loud noise in the hall wakes me again. I look at the alarm clock and it is 10 a.m. I have slept so long. I still feel feverish and weak. I go from being hot to cold. I cannot seem to get warm even though I am on fire. An odd smell drifts to my nose. I lift the sheets and see blood and a strange-colored discharge. This does not look normal. I better get dressed and go see the doctor, as I think I have an infection. I pull the desk chair over to help me stand and maneuver it to get to the bathroom to wash away the blood and discharge.

I forgo a shower for fear of fainting. I place several pads in a new pair of underwear and slide yesterday's dress on as it is close by. I will have the hotel clean the bed when I return. Grabbing the bag with my money, I slowly exit the room. I hold onto the side of the hallway wall to help get me to the elevator. Luckily, it is waiting, and the door opens immediately. I press the lobby button. Upon exiting, I see a tall umbrella by the hotel entrance and inquire if I may borrow it. The doorman gives me a strange look as the sun is shining, but he lets me take it. I use it as a cane to enable me to put one leg in front of the other. I walk slowly to the doctor's office. I can feel the pads are soaked with blood. I knock and Miss Paxon answers, peering through a hole in the door.

"June, do come in, Are you okay? You don't look good."

"I am not. I am bleeding and hot..."

No more words leave my mouth before I faint onto the floor.

When I come to, Dr. Adams is leaning over me on one side and the nurse on the other. I overhear their conversation and realize things are not good.

"It appears she has an infection and may be hemorrhaging. What's her fever?" the doctor asks the nurse.

"It was 102 when she arrived, and now it's 104. I have put cold compresses on her forehead and have put ice chips in bags around her body."

"This is not a good outcome. Let's start an IV to get fluid into her body to keep her hydrated. Let's put a light cover on her and lower the room temperature. Sponge her body with cool water. Repeat this every half hour. We need to break the fever and get it back to normal. Once she is more coherent, I'll do an internal examination to be sure nothing is amiss."

"Will do, Doctor. June, can you hear me? I'm going to put a needle in your forearm to inject some fluid. I want to take your temperature, so please open your mouth."

I hear a noise, a voice. It sounds like a female voice. "Mother, are you there? I am not feeling well, Mother."

"I see that. Please open your mouth for me."

"Ahhh."

"Good," the nurse says. "Please let the thing in your mouth sit there for a few minutes. I'm going to prick your forearm now. Good, I got the fluid started to help you feel better."

"Thank you, Mother. I am so sorry. I did not mean to be a bad daughter. I hope you and Father can forgive me. I love Peter so much. I just saw him."

"You did—where?"

"He was in a field, covered with blood and had no face or leg. I do not know what happened, but can you check if he is okay?"

"I will do so, rest and relax. We need to focus on you currently. Peter will be fine."

"Good, I'm glad, I am…." I pass out again.

Chapter 58
Negative Outcome—June 6, 1944

"Doctor, we're losing her. Her blood pressure is only 85 over 50. Her temperature is 105. She is unconscious and frighteningly pale."

"Her breathing is very shallow. I will start an infusion of water to keep her hydrated and am going to inject her with epinephrine."

"Look at me, June. Do you see me?" asks the nurse. The doctor opens the glass vial of epinephrine and fills a syringe. The nurse is holding my wrist. "Her pulse is over 120 and is weak."

The doctor injects the line with the adrenaline or epinephrine.

"She needs to go to a hospital," states the nurse.

"You know we can't take her to one. I could lose my medical license, and you would be banned from any future health care employment. We know abortions are risky. We haven't lost other patients; there's always a first."

"I hear you, but we need to act. She is not responding; her pulse is still shallow and high, and her blood pressure is now 80 over 48. Look at her knees and feet. They are blotchy and feel cool to the touch. Her breathing is increasing in pace but remains shallow. She's not going to last much longer."

"Let me try massaging her chest."

"June, are you able to hear me? If so, please blink your eyes. Doctor, there's slight eye movement; she is fading rapidly."

"I'm aware. I think we have done all we can for her. The massages—are they affecting her vitals in any way?"

"No, the pulse is a little lower, but she is still not responsive. Can we do more?"

"We need to replace fluids fast. Increase the rate of her IV."

I see Peter again, or at least I think it is him. He is on a beach—quite a distance from me. Now I can see a full face and a glow around his body. He seems to be walking toward me. Peter, come to me love. I have missed you so much. Wait, why are you walking away and waving for me to follow you? Slow down, I can't maintain your pace. Where are we going? Why the hurry? I'm coming as fast as I can; please wait for me.

That's better, I've caught up to you. Let me take your hand so we can walk together.

— ∞ —

"Time of death 4:43 p.m. on June 6, 1944," the doctor says remorsefully.

Miss Paxon can't look at him. Her eyes are focused on June. "I can't believe we lost her. She did so well during the procedure."

"I thought the same, but each patient is different," says Dr. Adams. "We had no prior medical history to go on. An infection is always a risk, and it appears June could not withstand the rigors of the procedure. I'm sorry this happened to her; she seemed so innocent. Let's take a moment of silence to honor her then we need to inform her parents."

"June gave me the contact information for sending a telegram to a local merchant who can reach her parents, as they do not have a telephone in the home. I'll get the information for you. I suggest you ask them to call you, as we need to respect her privacy. I sent them a telegram yesterday stating June had done well. I wish I hadn't."

"We need to keep our procedure confidential as well, so good advice. I'll send the message now while you prepare her for transport to a funeral director. I'll complete her death certificate, noting the cause of death as being an infectious complication following an operation."

"We need to retrieve her belongings from the hotel. I'll call to let them know June will not be returning and to gather what she may have left for me to get. I'll wear a wig and sunglasses, so I won't be easily recognizable when I retrieve her belongings and pay for her stay."

"Meanwhile, I'll contact a friend at the funeral home to see if there is a way her body can be stored until I get word of what her parents want to do with it."

Chapter 59
Notification—June 6, 1944
Reading, Pennsylvania

"Mr. Lehman, what do we owe the honor of your visit? It is so nice to see you," John says.

"I'm afraid I have an urgent message for you; may I come inside?"

"Why please do come in. Rebekah and I are finishing the plucking of a chicken."

"Hi Rebekah, good to see you and sorry for intruding," says Mr. Lehman.

"Why, you are not intruding at all. Would you like a fresh lemonade?"

"Thank you, but I need to get back to the store. I thought I should deliver this message in person; I received it through the wire. It is from a doctor in New York City. He wants you to call him as soon as possible. Here is his telephone number. I'm not sure why, as the telegram was brief."

"John, we need to call immediately. Mr. Lehman, could we use your telephone to do so and pay you for the call?" Rebekah asks.

"Sure, if you want, you can follow me to the store and call him from there. I think the sooner the better."

"Let us tell the children we are leaving and put this chicken in the icehouse," John replies.

"Sure thing. See you soon and again sorry for stopping by unannounced." Mr. Lehman opens the screen door to leave.

"You did us a favor; stop with the apologies. Thank you, and we will see you soon," Rebekah adds.

Once Mr. Lehman is out of earshot, Rebekah exclaims "Something is wrong, John. Why would we get a second telegram from the doctor? I knew this was the wrong thing to do. I am so worried and scared. Our poor June—I hope she is not suffering."

"Best not to jump to conclusions, Rebekah. Maybe the doctor wants to tell us June will be on her way home tomorrow. We need to remain calm until we hear otherwise."

"Well, I have a bad feeling and want to get to the store soon, so we can call before the doctor leaves for the day. I will tell the family we are going to go shopping; you can put the chicken on ice."

The store is empty of customers when we arrive. Mr. Lehman makes himself scarce to give us privacy while John places the call. "Hello, this is John Davis. I received a telegram to call this number."

"Yes, Mr. Davis. I'm Dr. Adams, the doctor who performed the operation on your daughter. I'm afraid I have bad news. June left this world today. She did great during the operation yesterday. This morning, she came back though with a high fever and stated she had been vomiting during the night. She looked extremely pale. These symptoms were signs of an infection. She also had uterine bleeding. We gave her medication and monitored her, but her blood pressure plummeted, while her heart raced. We tried to revive her, but she passed several hours later. I am so sorry to have to report this."

"I do not know what to say."

"I know this is a huge shock. I offer my sympathies to you and your family. June is the first patient to have passed following such an operation. We are upset ourselves. I do need to ask you some questions and give you information. As this call is costing you, I'll try and be as brief as possible. I recognize you will need to call me back once you have made some difficult decisions."

"Okay, go ahead."

"I understand you live in Pennsylvania. How would you like to transport June home? I suggest you contact a funeral director here—I can recommend one—to have her embalmed prior to transport. Since it is a distance, arrangements can be made with a train to bring her back to Pennsylvania. The train will need to be met by a funeral director on your end to accept a burial transit permit and the body. I will file a death certificate with the New York City Health Department. Since June died in New York, her death needs to be registered in this state, and not in Pennsylvania. We are attempting to get her belongings from the hotel and will include those with her body. I'm sure this is a lot to absorb. As you can imagine, time is of the essence, especially with getting her to a funeral home. Again, I can suggest one."

"This is a lot to think about. I am going to need tonight to think this over. Shall I call you again early tomorrow to review what we want to happen?"

"Yes, tomorrow morning will be fine. I will see if a funeral director friend will take her body now to keep it cool until we talk tomorrow. Please accept my deepest condolences. I will help however I can. Take care and we'll talk again in the morning."

"I will try. Thank you for letting us know. Goodbye."

"John, what is it? It is June, right? Please tell me; I am beside myself. You did not say a lot. Was it the doctor?"

"Rebekah, I think we should thank Mr. Lehman for letting us make the call and get into the truck before we discuss what the call was about."

"Mr. Lehman, are you close by? We have finished the call," John says.

"Great, I hope everyone is okay."

"They are for now, but I will need to make another call tomorrow morning, if I may. What do I owe you?"

"Why don't we wait until I get the phone bill? I'm not worried about getting paid."

"You are a great man, thank you so much. We will see you in the morning."

"John, we are in the truck, what is going on?" Rebekah says.

"You know God works in mysterious ways and often we do not understand them at the time. What I am about to tell you hurts me deeply and will change our lives. The call was from June's doctor. June did fine during the procedure; but the following day, she returned with a high fever. She had vomited over the night and had bleeding. The doctor did what he could, but she died this afternoon."

"Heavens, my daughter cannot be dead. She is a healthy girl. You are wrong. You must be wrong."

"Rebekah, I am upset also. I thought we were doing the right thing for her and us. I am filled with grief myself, and I am at a loss how to comfort you."

"We were doing the right thing?? How can you say that? I NEVER wanted her to abort the baby. I wanted her to have the child. Now I have lost my child. This is not God at work; this is not right. There must be a mistake. Maybe the doctor has the wrong woman in mind? Can we call him back."

"No, June is indeed gone from us. We must accept this. We should ask the Lord for forgiveness and keep our faith."

With tears rolling down her cheeks, Rebekah glances away and pounds the dashboard. "How could you take my daughter, Lord. She did not mean any harm. She was in love. And John, I hope I can forgive you at some point, but I cannot find it in my heart to do so right now. Your pride made us lose a precious child. I see no future without her."

"I am sorry, Rebekah, but we have a lot of decisions to make and quick ones, unfortunately. We need to get June back to Pennsylvania. We need to figure out what we are going to tell people. The doctor needs to know by tomorrow morning what to do with the body, as it decomposes rapidly. He gave me a lot of information. I need you to be rational and help me make several decisions."

"I need time. I cannot talk to you coherently right now. I suggest you drive us home and maybe by then, I can hear what you have to say. Right now, it is impossible for me to absorb any details or think about what we need to do. I need peace and quiet."

Once home, Rebekah asks Rachel if she would prepare the evening meal. "Father and I need to talk about something. Please go ahead and feed the rest of the family. He and I will grab a bite when we are ready."

"Happy to do so, Mother. Where are the groceries?"

"What? Oh, we did not shop for groceries. If you prepare the meal for tonight, it will be a big help. Father and I will be in the barn if you need us."

"What are we going to tell the children about June, Rebekah? I think we need to be as truthful as we can be. We said she was going to New York City for a couple of days to have an operation. Shall we tell them what the operation was for? They will mourn her loss and need some closure."

"If we tell them the whole truth, chances are word will spread about June's pregnancy. If that happens, we did lose June for nothing. It is best we say she got an infection after the operation, and her body could not fight it. That is not a lie; it just is not the complete truth. Whatever we say though is what we will need to be sure to tell other people. We need similar stories to stay afloat."

"How can you be so callous? Worrying about our stories. Can you at least admit to me you regret deciding to make her have the abortion? She would still be alive—pregnant, yes, but alive."

"Rebekah, I cannot express the grief I feel. I have been raised to be a stoic individual. That is what you are seeing. Inside, I am torn miles apart and am hurting deeply—like you are. I wanted to be a good father. In being one, I was delegated the responsibility of making difficult decisions. I did so, and it backfired. I am beyond sorry, but June is not coming back. She is gone, and we need to figure out what to do—and quickly."

"My heart is telling me I need to accept all of this, but it is hard. However, I will try and help you make decisions. I still need time, not measured by minutes, to adjust and absorb what has happened. I pray I will find peace soon. Go ahead, I know we need to get June's body. Can we send someone to get her?"

"The doctor recommended we use the train to transport her body. It would take at least four days for someone to drive from here to New York City and back. We need to bury her soon. The train can get here in a day. We need to arrange the train via a funeral director the doctor knows. This director will prepare a burial transit permit. It travels with the body and needs to be received by another funeral director on our end. We can use Ezra Parker, as he was who we used for our parents. I can contact him tomorrow before I call the doctor. We need to give his name to the doctor to give to the city funeral director. We need to plan June's burial and service. I want you to go with me to visit the bishop tomorrow to request he perform these, as I cannot ask Michael's father to do so."

"Sounds like you have it all figured out. The train is best. I want her returned as soon as possible. I think going with someone the doctor knows is smart for the city funeral director. Ezra would be who I would want to be the director on our end. I will gather June's white clothes for her to be buried in; we can put her in them once we get her back and get a wooden casket made. I will leave it to you to pay people.

"While I dread facing the bishop, I know we need to give June a proper burial. I will go with you to see the bishop tomorrow afternoon. I have ideas for what we should include in her service. We do need to meet with the family tonight. I am not hungry so I would like to talk with them after they finish their supper and are all together. I will let you tell them, so I do not offer information you do not want shared. Once Ezra and the bishop are told, there is no telling what gossip will spread among the members of our meetinghouse. The children need time to prepare. We need to tell them now."

"You are correct. I will make the visits tomorrow, and place the call. But right now, we need to talk with our children."

Chapter 60
Saying Farewell—June 10, 1944

"Today we are gathered in the Davis house to honor their daughter, June, who left his world to join her Savior," states the bishop. "This is a bittersweet moment, as June should have had many more years of life. God works in mysterious ways though, and it is not for us to question when he calls his people home. June is resting in heaven without earthly cares or concerns. She earned this reward through her faith to the Lord and her gracious behavior. She always was willing to help others and was a regular attendee of our meetinghouse services. I recall her harmonious voice; it blended well with others, as did June.

"An early death is difficult for those who remain. May we say a prayer for God to give strength and courage to her parents, John and Rebekah, and to her siblings—Rachel, Aaron, Mary, Jacob, Martha, and Thomas.

Dear Heavenly Father,

We come to you to thank you for welcoming June into eternity. May she be at peace. We ask you to look favorably upon her parents and siblings, as they make sense of their loss and its impact on the family. May each person gain the capacity to deal with his or her loss in his own time and way. Keep them safe and strong in the Faith, as they progress through their grief. Thank you, Lord, for giving us your son, so we can live eternally.

Blessed is your name.

Amen

"Let us rise and sing one of June's favorite hymns, "Amazing Grace.""

"Please be seated. I would like to say a few words about June's life followed by a sermon on the topic she most favored—humbleness. You all are welcome to join the procession to the cemetery, where June will be laid to her permanent earthly rest."

The service lasts less than an hour. Many members of the Faith travel to the freshly hand-dug gravesite. Several help to carry the wooden casket—built by neighbors—containing June's body. A short gravesite ceremony occurs. More people are present at this ceremony than the funeral service, as it is open to Faith members and the public. The weather is beautiful—sunny and warm, with a calm wind. As people leave, they offer their condolences to the family. One couple to do so surprises Rebekah; it is the Brandts—Peter's parents.

"We are so sorry about the loss of your daughter, Rebekah and John. It is a difficult thing to understand, why God takes some from us so young—and usually the good ones. While we never met June, we heard about her from our son Peter, who never talked to us about any other girl. I want to let him know she has passed, but it is hard to send such sad news to our boys who see death daily. While I feel Peter would want to know, I will wait to tell him, as I don't want to upset him while he's fighting. Rebekah, could I pull you aside for a moment?"

Bertha pulls me out of hearing distance from John, Ralph, and the children.

"Again, let me extend our deepest sympathies for the loss of your cherished daughter. Arthur, Ralph's brother at the feed mill told us about June's death. I feel we have lost someone also, from hearing about her from Peter. That's why we wanted to meet you in person and attend June's service. I'm sure Peter would be attending and sharing his feelings about June with you himself; but we don't know where he is, except for somewhere in Europe. I fear for him daily. This war is not good, but I'm glad he has June to think of when he is lonely. It will be a terrible loss to him to know she is gone. My heart, my husband's, and Peter's are with you and your remaining family. Cherish your memories. I would like to meet soon, as I have something to share with you at a more sensible time."

"Well, thank you for your kindness and support. I appreciate the long distance you have traveled to convey your sympathy. It is beyond difficult losing a child such as June, who was sweet, inquisitive, and mostly obedient to us and the Lord. I accept your invitation to continue our conversation, as I would like to get to know you better. When are you returning to Georgia?"

"We are going to return in a couple of weeks. Meanwhile, we are staying with Ralph's brother. They haven't seen each other in quite a while, and it's been nice getting reacquainted with him and his wife."

"In that case, please stop by the house for coffee some morning before you leave."

"Wonderful. And sorry, I didn't mean to monopolize your time. You have others wanting to converse with you now. I look forward to our upcoming chat, and God bless you and your lovely family."

Chapter 61
Tension—June 10, 1944
Rebekah

The Davis family silently rides home in a horse and buggy, which is traditional transport for Plain funerals. Upon arrival, the children rapidly head to the house to change into their daily clothes.

"May we go to the barn for a moment? Rebekah asks John.

"Okay, I need to dismantle the horses from the buggy anyway and clean them. Care to help me?"

"Let me change my clothes, and I will meet you in the barn."

As I slip out of my good Sunday dress, I rehearse what I am about to say to John. The service was too much for me to bear; it brought me no comfort. We are living a lie—a big one. The meetinghouse members were so empathetic about the loss of our daughter, but little do they know the real reason for her death. Also, I am troubled by the request from Peter's mother to talk with her privately. Does she know? How could she? I am struggling with my emotions and my sense of what is right and wrong. I will express my thoughts to John about our talking to the bishop. We need to seek forgiveness at whatever the cost. I cannot live with myself, and knowing John as I do, I believe he is struggling also with this horrible secret. We made the wrong choice; I need repentance to move forward. I will not mention Bertha's request until I know more what she wants to talk with me about. With these musings, I descend the stairs and head toward the barn, preparing myself for a confrontation with my husband.

"Here is a comb, Rebekah, to help clean the mud from the horses, and a body brush to use once you have the thick mud removed. I will pick their hooves and detangle their tails. We can work together on brushing their tangled manes. I thought today's service was a nice sendoff for June. A lot of meetinghouse members attended, more than I expected. She had many friends who paid her respect. What are your thoughts on the service?"

"That is why I wanted to talk. I agree the service was well done and appreciate the sentiments expressed by our fellow meetinghouse members. June deserved a nice farewell. The whole time though I was aching inside, feeling like a liar to these virtuous individuals. We are deceiving them by not telling the truth, John. We are deceiving ourselves by thinking we can get away with this lie for the rest of our lives. I, for one, cannot go on. I normally do not tell you what to do, but in this case, I am issuing a jussive statement. I want to go together to meet with the bishop and tell him the truth. My soul needs to rest, and it cannot while this lie remains."

"Rebekah, I am trying so hard to keep myself under control. Do you think I enjoy lying to peers and the bishop? Please realize if we do come forth with the truth, we will lose a lot. We potentially could lose our children if they wish to remain in the Faith. We will be removed from the meetinghouse and will be shunned by our friends and other families. Is this what you want?"

"Of course this is not what I want. What I want is meaningless; what I need is to remain sane. We need to confess, John, I cannot stand this much longer. Deceit is horrible."

"You have got to promise me you will not tell anyone. Look at me, Rebekah. We made a decision. There is a lot at stake here; we need to remain silent. Promise me you will."

"I cannot offer you this promise, but my marital vow to you requires I honor your wishes. You have another month to think through all of this. I will go to the bishop alone then, if need be."

"Bless you. Please pray with me. I want no more harm to come our way. I want us to honor June with our silence, as it will affect her lasting reputation if word gets out about her promiscuousness and being an unwed mother. I will count on you to give me this coming month to reflect."

Chapter 62
Meet Up—June 15, 1944

"Thank you for meeting with me, Rebekah," Bertha says. "I thought it was best we meet outside our homes and am glad you agreed to ride with me to town for coffee instead. I hope you have had some respite from June's passing. You have been in my thoughts and prayers."

"Kind of you, Bertha. I thought being a mother was hard enough, but I would never wish the pain I have been feeling on anyone. Nature's intent is for parents to die first, and now I know why."

"May I give you a hug. I know we don't know each other well, but I feel for you and wish to console you. I wanted to talk for several reasons. One, to let you know Ralph, Peter and I care about your loss. Peter called me and wrote in a letter how he was falling deeply in love with June. He has never felt this way about another girl. I want you to know how much she was loved by my son. If he were here, I'm sure he would have been at her burial and would be mourning her passing. He is a caring person.

"I have not written to Peter about June's passing, as I mentioned earlier. He needs to know, but I am worried about the impact this news will have on him while he is fighting. There's a reason for my concern. In his letter, he alluded to a clandestine meeting with June the night before he left for England. They apparently met in a hay mow to talk about his leaving, as he was forbidden by John to see her publicly. He didn't come right out and say this, but my guess is with their youthful hormones and emotions of his pending departure, they may have had a sexual union. I would not have blamed them, but I guess in your Faith, it is judged as wrong. I am personally glad he has this memory of June, if indeed this is the case. Men need an anchor to keep them alive while fighting for our country. And if they did explore each other, I am glad it was with someone like June, who seemed like a good woman."

"Oh dear, I am glad we are sitting," Rebekah says. "June knew John was against her seeing Peter. You are right though. Our Faith frowns on sex outside of marriage. Your shared words of Peter's love for June helps me to know he is a good man. You should feel proud he is fighting for our country, although I am sure it is hard on you to not know what exactly he is facing every day."

"No truer words have been spoken. I fear for him and pray daily God will see him through this. I think he only has a couple of months left to serve. I am planning a town parade to welcome him home and hope you, John, and your family will attend. It would mean a lot to Peter to have you represent June. By then, he will know she is gone."

"Peter should be greeted and thanked by our community. I realize he could have opted not to serve in the war by declaring his assistance with farming. It is admirable he felt compelled to fight and not get deferred. We owe him and men like him even though our Faith does not believe in war."

"Yes, we do, and you are right, he made a choice to serve. He needs to come home, as we need help with the farm and butcher shop. Now tell me how your other children are doing."

The conversation continued for some time as Rebekah highlighted each child's accomplishments, their acceptance of June's passing, and her wishes for their futures. Bertha reciprocated with news about her children.

"Before we go, I have one last sensitive thing I wish to chat with you about, Rebekah. If Peter sired a child with June, I hope it was not terminated. I know June died of complications of an operation. It seems strange to me she went to New York City for the operation, when there are great physicians nearby, especially in Philadelphia or Baltimore. I hope a grandchild of mine was not wasted due to religious reasons. You don't have to tell me; I'll leave you with this parting thought. I know how youth can be and having sex is not a true sin in our belief system. Killing a fetus is not either. However, if it was my grandchild's fetus that was harmed, I'll never be able to forgive you."

"That is a lot to put on me, Bertha. I cannot confirm your conjecture. Oh dear, look at the time; I need to get home to cook supper. Thank you for the coffee."

"Apologies if my words have upset you. I mainly wanted you to know Peter loves, or loved, June. I am sharing this information to provide you with some kind of assurance of his honor. He is a good son and a kind man."

"Yes, I am sure he is both. I know the planned homecoming festivities will be grand. We will try to be present. I would like to see Peter and thank him in person."

"Waiter, check please. This is on me, Rebekah."

"Thank you for your time and generosity, Bertha. I appreciate the ride." What Bertha does not realize is what a ride she put me on. Between her questioning and a letter recently received from my sister, I do not see how we can continue to lie about June's death.

Chapter 63
Pressure—June 15, 1944

"Where are the children, John?" Rebekah asks.

"They are playing outside. Why?"

"Good, we need to talk. I know I promised you I would not go to the bishop until you had some time to contemplate what we should do, but two things have arisen forcing the timing to be sooner."

"Whatever could they be?"

"First, here is a letter from my sister.

June 9, 1944

Dear Sister Rebekah & family,

The sad news was received this morning and indeed cannot tell the sadness I have been laboring under all day. Oh, that I might pour out my grief in bitter tears. "Why?" I cannot tell why, but I feel that I want to and be relieved not that I would wish Dear June into this world again. The thought comes to me again and again she has overcome the world all trials, all sorrows, and all sufferings. Oh, what a comfort this should be to us and is, but it is hard to part with our friends. Though it be only for a few days, only a few years at the longest. Seems we are called over one by one soon we shall be as one family in that beautiful home if we prove faithful.

Oh, that I might have a comforting word for you all. I know how much she will be missed as a dear June as a dear Sister. She will be missed everywhere but a conciliating thought that has only gone home, soon we will go to meet her. The Lord has a wise purpose in it which of course we don't understand, and the future alone sometimes reveals to us. Though we cannot understand now, the future may show to you what has been meant by it. I don't know who wrote the letter about June's death. There was no name to it. But it was stated that you want to honor the Lord for his care over you as a family. Oh, I was so glad for these words I thought no difference what comes to the Christians he feels and sees the love of God in it all…

Did June seem to be impressed with the thought that she might not get well, and did she have a desire to leave this world? Did she suffer much pain before and after the operation? Was she conscious until the last or don't you know? There are so many things that come to my mind, and I think I must know. I wondered many times since we heard of your trouble why are we so far apart. I wished more than ever that we could be together but so it is only so we can meet-in the home beyond is my prayer. Dear Rebekah, I do not know if you have given your heart to the Lord or not. If not, I hope you may hear the loud call and give your heart to the Lord. Time is short. The Christian life is such a happy life and a comfort when we come to leave this world. Will prepare you to meet your only dear sister. With this I close, hoping to hear from you soon. Please write soon.

Your affectionate Sister,

Ruth

"You can read between the lines her suspicion about June's death. She knows me well and has interpreted the lack of sharing details with her as odd. She will continue to inquire about what happened; I know her. Second, I had coffee with Peter's mother today."

"I did not know you were going to meet Bertha. Are they still in town? When did this come about?"

"Bertha asked me when she pulled me aside at the graveyard. She said she wanted to share some information with me. They are staying with the owner of the feed mill, Ralph's brother, Arthur and his wife. He is how they learned about June's death and decided to attend her funeral.

"Bertha drove me to town today to chat. I should have told you sooner, but I figured it would be a friendly talk. It was mostly, except for one thing. Peter had talked with her about his forbidden love for June and had subsequently written to her about his deepening love for June when he was in bootcamp. He mentioned he had seen June before he left for Europe; they met in our barn. Bertha was not sure, but she believes, by reading through the lines of a letter, Peter and June may have united during this visit. She seems to be wondering if June's trip to New York City for an operation was to end the life of a conceived child. She said she was okay with premarital sex and abortions in principle, but if we had done away with her grandchild, she would never forgive us. Her words hurt me to no end.

"Apparently, Peter's time in Europe is almost over. Bertha is planning a welcome home event with a parade and invited us to attend. Peter knows the truth, John. Maybe not about the baby, but about the chance a life could have been created the evening prior to his departure. We need to go to the bishop now for guidance. I will go without you if need be. I am sorry, but we will soon be exposed, and I would rather confess first."

"This does put pressure on us. Your sister has always been nosey. If she catches any wind of a possible baby, there is no telling what she will do. Peter's return could reveal our lie. He will want to know the details of why June died and where. I still think we have some time though to reflect. When is Peter expected home?"

"Bertha did not say exactly, but it sounded like in a couple of months. I know she is not going to write him now and tell him about June's death, as she feels this would be hard on him. She is afraid that the news would affect him mentally. My guess is she will wait a little longer, so the news is closer to the time of his return or wait until his return. I would do the latter if I were her."

"Sounds as if we have some time."

"No, John, I need this off my chest soon. I will contact the bishop if you do not by the end of this week."

"You are giving me no choice. I want to be present when you talk to the bishop. Maybe between both of us, we can make him understand the situation we were in and why we made the choices we did. I will request a meeting with him tomorrow. It is already Thursday, and he is preparing for the Sunday service, so our meeting will not be until next week."

"Thank you. I am feeling a little better knowing this deceit will soon be exposed. I cannot bear the pressure."

Chapter 64
Bertha's Letter to Peter

June 18, 1944

My Dear Peter,

How are you? I hope well and O.K. We are reading and listening to lots of news and we often wonder if you are in some of these things, we hope not.

Well, it seems it takes lots of work and labor and blood shed to hit the Germans. Well, God is on the throne, and he will not let wrong rule. It must be right. Well, your cousin and wife were here today, and did they ever have lots of fun. Your cousin washed his car and then he and your sister turned the hose on each other and they had a good cooling off. Well, we have our paper all on but the small room and cellar way, and I expect to have it painted. I painted some of the floors and got it pretty well fixed up – some things upstairs yet to do. But I surely had a time till we got the old logs sawed off and put new timber in and cut doors and windows and tore off plastering and now it is all painted. It looks nice. I know you will like it or else it will be funny. I have one room yet and a stairway to do yet, but that will have to wait till the cherries and raspberries and harvest is past and my gardens worked. My peeps are doing pretty good. Your cousin took some eggs along to Va. for himself and something went along with him for his wife...

Dad says all plans are for your home coming and I hope it will be soon over and I don't think I can let you out of my sight for awhile…Your last letter was dated May 7th.

Well Good Bye,
Mother

— ∞ —

Reading, Pennsylvania

John says, "Rebekah, I stopped by the store today and Mr. Lehman handed me this. He said it was in a letter from Peter asking him to deliver it to June."

He hands me the envelope containing a V-mail letter addressed to June. Shaking, I rip open the flap and remove the letter. Tears stream as I read what Peter wrote to June. The only words able to escape my lips are "He did love her."

John snatches the letter from me to read it himself. He drops his head and profusely bawls. I enfold him in my arms until his energy is spent. He collapses onto a chair. The look on his face illustrates true misery. "Peter would have made an honest woman of June. He cared and committed himself to her. We were so wrong."

Chapter 65
Confession—June 27, 1944

"Thank you, Bishop for meeting with me and Rebekah today."

"It is always a pleasure to see the two of you. What can I do for you?"

"We have come today to confess a major sin. It is my sin. I take full responsibility for it. Rebekah should not be held accountable for it."

"You have aroused my interest, please proceed."

"I had to make a difficult decision as the head of our family. My intent was to cause the least amount of harm to the family. My actions have proven to place us in greater danger, and I am indeed regretful."

"Repentance is good. Realizing when you need to do so is a good sign. What did you do?"

"You know we recently lost our child June to an operation with a bad outcome."

"Yes, I am aware, as I helped to officiate her funeral service."

With difficulty John continues. "Well, the operation was not one blessed by God according to our Faith."

"I see. Let me guess, June had an abortion."

"Yes, she did not want to, so her soul should not be held in contempt. I forced her to have it. Even my wife did not wish this to happen."

"Why did you ask June to do this?"

"After weighing all options, I thought this would be a way for her to save face, and for the rest of our children not to be harassed or harmed by the thoughts and comments of others. I know how cruel youth can be to one another. I was not sure how strong June's love was for the father and vice versa, and if he would do the right thing and marry her."

"Did you ask him to wed her?"

"I could not, as he is fighting in Europe."

"Oh, a military soldier. This makes it worse, as you know we do not believe in war. Peace is our goal."

"Yes, we believe in pacifism also. However, before this young man left for Europe, he and June physically united. The emotion of going to fight and the possibility of not returning I am sure drove the passion. I heard later Peter called and wrote his mother to express his love for June. This information was shared with me after the decision was made to abort the baby. Previously, I had forbidden June to get romantically involved, as the boy was not of our Faith. He even asked me for permission to court and I declined. They both knew their love was forbidden. Yet, they had sex out of wedlock."

"Why did you not seek counsel earlier?"

"My thought was to keep you from knowing about it and having to act. If the abortion would have gone smoothly, June would have returned to life as normal, and no one would be wiser."

"This is interesting. As the leader of our community's faith, I have to say you have indeed committed several sins. First, you aborted a fetus that would have become an individual. In our Faith, this is equivalent to killing. Second, you lied about it to me, the church elders, fellow Faith members, relatives, and to your remaining children, as my guess is you have not told them the real reason for June's death. Third, you have put Rebekah in a tenuous situation by asking her to lie with you. She is guilty now by default. I do not know who else you have asked to lie about this, but my suspicion is the doctor who performed the operation illegally, as abortion is not legal in either Pennsylvania or surrounding states."

Hanging his head in intense shame, John acknowledges these lies are true by shaking his head up and down. "You are correct. I have sinned and I am ready to suffer the consequences. Please give Rebekah amnesty. She only went along with me due to my insistence. Because I am the father of our household, she had no choice but to conform to my wishes. Please do not punish her for my sins."

"This is a difficult situation. Normally, for most sins, I would ask the elders of the Faith to vote for you to be excommunicated. If they agree, a vote would then be conducted by the entire congregation. With the intensity of the sins you committed though, I will ask only the elders to vote for an immediate shunning of you. This means I need to share the details, so they can make the appropriate vote. If shunned, you are not welcome to return to this meetinghouse or any other of our Faith. It means you may not ask for rides with other meetinghouse members nor accept goods from them. You may not break bread with them. I see regret within you for what you have done; but due to the intensity of the sins, you will not be welcomed back if the vote is in favor of shunning.

"Rebekah, since you bowed to your husband's decisions, you will not be voted on. Understand this means you and John cannot live together if he is shunned. John cannot see you or the children or take part in any family events or activities. He still needs to provide for you. You have a choice though. You can decide to be shunned as well. This would allow you to remain together as a family. However, none of you would be welcome in the Faith.

"I need to ask how you feel about all of this, Rebekah? Do you wish to keep the Faith and be separated from your husband?"

"Dear Bishop, we recognize we have put you in a predicament, and as John mentions, we are willing to suffer the consequences. I am not willing to have my family taken away from me. I vowed to love John through sickness and health and through all of life's tribulations. My wish is to remain faithful to him. We brought beautiful children into this world. I want to be a part of their lives for the remainder of my time here on earth."

"Even if this means you too will be shunned by others in the Faith?" the bishop asks.

"Even with this understanding. We have sinned and paid the price through the loss of our daughter. No other earthly punishment can be as harsh. Our souls have been impacted by our loss and our poor judgments. We will never be the same. I do not want my children to be taunted by others for actions John and I took. They will come with us; in fact, I wish to say I am no longer interested in staying in the Faith. I want to break free and start a new life. John and I have discussed this, and he agrees. No vote is needed, as we are giving you our resignation from the Plain Faith. You can say what you wish to the congregation."

"Well, this is a drastic measure. Please be sure you will not regret it. Once you leave, there is no returning," the bishop declares.

"Rebekah states it well," John confirms. "We hereby renounce our Plain Faith and wish you and all the meetinghouse members our best. Thank you."

Chapter 66
Beyond Shunned—June 27, 1944

"Life is going to be different for us," John says to Rebekah. "Thank you for supporting me today. We need to keep the farm; it is our livelihood. I will have to see about getting the children enrolled in regular school this fall. To prevent them from being ridiculed, I suggest we dress them in normal clothes. It is hard to believe we are not Plain anymore. I guess we need to talk about what religion we wish to become. We need to accept our Plain friends will not be permitted to associate with us. New friends will need to be made."

"Indeed, this is a new life for us. Through confessing to the bishop, I feel we have atoned for our sin of lying and of being deceitful. It is hard to start over, but I no longer have nightmares about being caught in our untruths. A feeling of relief and calm has come over me. Thank you for going to the bishop. It was hard to do, I know, but it was necessary."

"Rebekah, we need to talk with the children soon about what has happened, so they are able to transition to a new life with us. I am so relieved you have forgiven me and will continue to be my life partner. If you had decided otherwise, I would not have blamed you. My love for you is stronger, and I know together we can face whatever comes our way. There will be many obstacles we will conquer together. Partner, I cherish what we have retained, and may we grow with what we will experience together in our new future. We have June's reputation to uphold as well; she deserves our backing. Rumors will spread and we need to try and squelch them. We can create a new way of life for our family, I know we can."

"It will be so different. I feel our first order of business is to visit with several pastors to see if we can be accepted into a new faith. Our beliefs are what steered us in the past and should be our beacon in the future. Is there a religion you think we should explore?"

"Rebekah, I think our best approach is to visit with different ministers and see what we think about what they say and how open they are to accepting our situation. I have learned the hard way to be truthful going forward. Truth will be our main shared value. If some people cannot handle our truth, we need to seek those who can. Our reasoning for June having an abortion was to avoid being shunned. Now that we are, our worst fear is over. We lost what we held unto dearly; but now having lost it, I feel relief. There is no more hiding the reality of what we did to protect our family. Our family is still ours except for having lost June. We need to be confident when we talk with them about the future. They need to see our strength, so they are not negatively affected by the past. They deserve our guidance and love."

"One thing I would like to do is to reach out to Peter's mother. I feel she needs to know the truth. I hope she can forgive us even though she said she could not if we had gotten rid of her grandchild. My heart is still heavy when I think of this. I need to make things right with her."

"Do what you must. Hopefully, Bertha will come to understand we were trying to protect June. She is a mother, after all. I give you my blessing to talk with her."

"All of this makes me dizzy; there is so much to do. Let us make a list of things and a plan of attack on how to accomplish each thing. This would help me get through all of this."

"I agree. Together we can itemize and prioritize the activities. First thing though is to talk with our children. Let us set family time for tomorrow night once supper is over. I will go tell them now."

"Thank you, John. I love you; we need each other to get through all of this."

Chapter 67
Turn of Events—July 6, 1944
Rebekah

Calling Bertha is not going to be easy. She was clear how upset she would be if she found out June had had an abortion. With all that has transpired over the last month, I need to set things right with her. She should know the truth, as she would have been the grandmother of June and Peter's child. John takes me to the general store to place the call.

When I reach the Brandt home telephone, Ralph answers. I inquire if Bertha is available to chat. I hear her crying in the background. "It's not the best time to talk, Rebekah," Ralph replies.

"I am sorry. I can call back."

There is rustling in the background. Bertha gets on the telephone; her voice is raspy. "Rebekah, we just received a telegram. It says…" Ralph finishes reading it. The telegram informs them of Peter's death. He was killed in battle.

I ask for Bertha to be put back on the phone; she loses control and sobs. I do not know what to say; I try to console her.

Momentarily, she states, "We knew this was a possibility when Peter enlisted, but the shock of the truth is too much to bear. He is dead; our son is dead."

"I am so sorry. It is not easy to lose a child."

"Of course, you have lost one. I didn't mean to be callous. Do you ever get over it—the loss, I mean? Peter was such a good person. He can't be dead. We were planning his homecoming. It was going to be joyful and memorable—with a parade to honor his dedication to our country. Now there is nothing."

"Please accept my deepest sympathy. While I did not know Peter well, the fact my daughter loved him indicates to me he had to be special. I know his loss is new to you and hard to comprehend. I can say the unbearable pain diminishes with time. You can be proud of your son. He gave his life to save our freedom. He is a hero."

Time seems to drag, second by second. I try to think of other things to say. Obviously, now is not the time to talk about the abortion and June's death. They will have to wait. Bertha seems eager to talk more about Peter, so I let her.

"Thank you for calling Rebekah. I'm sure you had a purpose for your call. I'm so sorry, what did you want to talk with me about?" Bertha inquires.

"It can wait for another day. There's no rush, but if we can help meanwhile, do not hesitate to ask." I end the call and share the sad news with John and Mr. Lehman.

Epilogue

Life continued for the Davis and Brandt families. The Davis family stayed on their homestead and continued to raise horses, cows, pigs, and chickens. They tried several churches in the area and eventually decided not to join one church, but to frequent many. Their faith remained a constant in their family's life. All of the children got married, giving John and Rebekah a total of 19 grandchildren.

Determined to not let Peter's death be in vain, the Brandt's held a town parade in Decatur to honor Peter posthumously. His body was flown home from France, and he was buried at his parents' expanded future gravesite. An official letter from the War Department was issued on July 8, 1944, confirming Peter's death.

July 8, 1944

Dear Mr. and Mrs. Brandt:

It is with regret that I am writing to confirm the recent telegram informing you of the death of your son, Private First Class Peter R. Brandt, 33,500,043, Infantry, who was killed in action on 6 June 1944 in France.

I fully understand your desire to learn as much as possible regarding the circumstances leading to his death and I wish there were more information available to give you. Unfortunately, reports of this nature contain only the briefest details as they are prepared under battle conditions, and the means of transmission are limited.

I know the sorrow this message has brought you and it is my hope that in time the knowledge of his heroic service to his country, even unto death, may be of sustaining comfort to you.

I extend to you my deepest sympathy.

Sincerely yours,

J.A. Ulio

Major General

The Adjutant General

— ∞ —

Peter received a bronze star medal, complete with an accompanying citation. The citation included brief details of the heroic measures Peter had taken to cover for his fellow soldiers on the Colleville-sur-Mer Beach, Normandy, France. He was one of two BAR (Browning Automatic Rifle) gunners, who exited a Landing Craft, Vehicle, Personnel (LCVP aka Higgins Boat) to enter the knee-high ocean water, only to be hit by mortar and machine-gun fire. He lost his leg due to a shell fragment.

The local newspaper recorded acknowledgement of the bronze star honor.

Citation of Bronze Star Medal Award

Ralph Brandt's Received it for Their Son, Pfc. Brandt

Mr. and Mrs. Ralph Brandt, Decatur, Georgia, have received the citation the Bronze Star medal awarded their son, Pfc. Peter R. Brandt, who was killed in action on D-Day, June 6, 1944 in France. The citation reads as follows:

"Peter R. Brandt, private first class, company F. 16th Infantry, for heroic achievement in connection with military operations against the enemy in the vicinity of Colleville-sur-Mer, Normandy, France, June 6, 1944. Realizing that he was facing certain death, Pfc. Brandt remained on exposed beach and, by directing effective automatic rifle fire upon enemy gun emplacements, enabled his section to maneuver into strategic positions. In the performance of his heroic, self-imposed mission, Pfc. Brandt was mortally wounded. Residence at enlistment: Reading, Pennsylvania. Next of kin: Mr. and Mrs. Ralph Brandt, father and mother, R.R.1, Decatur, Georgia."

Pfc. Brandt entered the service on January 10, 1944, and received his basic training at Camp Butner, North Carolina. He left this country for foreign duty on March 27, 1944, and was stationed in England until the time of the invasion.

The following poem was sent by WAC Sgt. Wendy Goodman, now stationed in New Guinea, to Mr. and Mrs. Brandt and family:

"I cannot say, and I will not say
That he was dead. He is just away!
With a cheery smile, and a wave of the hand,
He has wandered into an unknown land.
And left us dreaming how very fair
It needs must be, since he lingers there.
And yon – O you who the wildest yearn
For the old-time step and the glad return.
Think of him faring on, as dear
In the love of There as the love of Here;
Think of him still as the same,
I say:
He is not dead – he is just away."

Peter's two siblings got married and produced seven grandchildren. Ralph died five years after Peter. Bertha

received payments from Peter's Veteran's Administration-
issued life insurance policy of $10,000 for the rest of her life.
When she learned of the $71.50 monthly payment, she
commented she was going to live a long life to make Peter pay
for enlisting. She lived to be over 80 years old.

NOTICE OF SETTLEMENT

National Service Life Insurance

To: Mr. & Mrs. Ralph Brandt   *Date: November 14, 1944*

Decatur, Georgia   *Name: Brandt, Peter R.*

XC – 3,638,151

N – 8,960,526

*You are hereby notified that, a beneficiary of insurance in the
amount of $10,000.00 granted to Peter R. Brandt, by the United States
under the National Service Life Insurance Act of October 8, 1940, as
amended, you are entitled to monthly payments of $71.50 beginning June
6, 1944 to continue for life.*

*The initial payment under this settlement will be dispatched to
you at the earliest possible date. If you should change your address, the*

Accounting Division, Finance Service, Veterans Administration,
Washington 25, D.C. must be immediately notified.

All future communications with reference to this case must bear
the File Number XC-3,638,151.

Very truly yours.
H.L. McCoy
Director of Insurance

Peter's sister desired more information about Peter's death and in the hopes of learning more, contacted another soldier's parents, one who had been killed the same day. They lived in North Carolina. The families stayed in contact over the years.

West Asheville, NC
December 9ᵗʰ, 1944

Dear Miss Brandt:

We received your kind and welcome letter some few days ago and was so good to hear from you and to know you all are well. We are well at the present but very lonely and lonesome, as we miss our dear boy and his sweet letters so much. It hurts us so bad and doesn't seem like we can ever stand it and we know you feel the same about your dear brother. We look at their sweet pictures dozens and dozens of time each day and they are so sweet to give up. No, we haven't had any details about our boy yet but want to so bad. We wrote the chaplain and the Com.-officer of his company about 60 days ago, but so far have not had any reply. We will let you know if we do hear... If you hear about your brother as how he was killed, please let us know. We hear from our other sweet boy quite often he is still in Calif. He wants to come home for Christmas so bad but says they won't let him come, and it seems so hard for us. So, we will close by saying please write us, as we enjoy reading your nice letters so much and you all seem so dear to us.

Wishing you a very Merry Christmas and a Happy New Year. Goodbye and Best Wishes.

Sincerely,
Mr. and Mrs. Dane

— ∞ —

Seventy-five years after the battle, Peter's army dog tags and mess kit were returned. No one knows the long journey they traveled, and what they saw along the way—from France to Decatur, Georgia.

Through the death of their children, Bertha and Rebekah became good friends. Their shared grief created a unique bond between them. Rebekah confessed about the abortion in time.

She sent Bertha the letter June had written Peter the night before the abortion, unread. She had found it among June's belongings returned from the hotel.

With other grandchildren, Bertha was able to forgive John and Rebekah. She was a source of information for Rebekah about how to live as a non-Plain woman. Numerous letters and visits were shared among the two families, even though they were not physically close. It was as if Peter and June's love joined the two families together in their absence.

Piecing together the two histories, the families realized Peter and June died on the same day—June 6, 1944. They decided to call this date the anniversary date for their starstruck lovers, even though no wedding had ever taken place. It was the day both families suffered a major loss; one not realizing it until almost a month later due to delayed government communications. This day would be honored through time as it was Operation Overlord or D-Day; one of the most deadly and memorable battles of World War II.

Afterword

No one in our extended family knows how much of the story I have written is true.

A young female relative of the Plain Faith traveled to a large city for an operation in 1893 and died at the age of 25 as a result. Her father had passed prior to the operation, so who made the decision about the operation is unknown. From letter addresses, I was able to locate the building where the operation took place, which was not a hospital, but an office building. I was able to identify the doctor and several surgical books he authored. He was a eugenics advocate, which made his prestigious alma mater university reject his attempted donations to the institution. How my family chose this doctor remains a mystery, as do the logistics of how my female relative traveled to the big city from rural Pennsylvania.

A male relative, my uncle, died on D-Day, fighting on Omaha Beach, Normandy, France, as part of the 1st U. S. Army Infantry Division.

These two relatives lived a generation apart. Letters, written by them and others, have been saved and transferred among the family. Several are transcribed in this book.

Liberties were taken to create one story of love from the merciless evils of war and the cruel judgements of religion. Only Peter and June know for sure what happened and what led to their ominous loss of dignity in the eyes of some. Their silent footsteps echo throughout the years as their short lives are not forgotten. May their tragic stories provide guidance.

Acknowledgements

I want to thank my village who was there for me as I wrote and published this novel. The first person is my long-term friend, Taffy Beach, who traveled the journey with me, as she wrote her *Manatee Bay Cozy Mystery Series*. It was wonderful to have her as a sounding board, an editor, a confidante, a guide, and a fellow trailblazer. We learned so much together. In addition, many within my local community offered their time to read my drafts and make suggestions for improvements to make the story richer—thank you Susan Murnane, Leigh Hume, Ann De Jong Hodgson, and Felice De Jong. And special appreciation to my friends who volunteered to read my novel and provide valuable feedback—Betsy Haller, Cherie Blazer, Jana Campbell Goetz, Carol Self, Donna Flake, and Linda Williams. Most of all, mega thanks to my husband, Mark, who let me talk ad nauseam about my plans, the plot, the challenges, and the joys of writing. Your never-ending support and love mean the world to me.

About the Author

This is Jean Shipman's first novel joining two other professionally edited books on the subjects of innovation and collaborations within health sciences libraries. Jean is from a small town in Pennsylvania and has family connections to the Plain religion. She was a medical librarian for about 40 years, a profession she chose based on her desire to move to a city. Much of the story for *One Tragic June* originates from her mother's family history and letters transferred over time (many are included in the book). Jean lives in the foothills of Virginia with her husband, Mark, and cat.

Join her on Facebook bit.ly/4nRLn06

Book Club Guide
Jean Pugh Shipman

Thank you for choosing *One Tragic June* for your book club discussion. This story, inspired by real letters and true experiences, invites readers to reflect on faith, love, conscience, and the quiet courage that endures even in the shadows of war. Use the questions below to spark thoughtful conversation and have fun learning.

Discussion Questions

1. **Authenticity of history**: How did the inclusion of real letters and true stories affect your emotional connection to the novel? Did it make the characters feel more real? What role do letters play in preserving truth, love, or misunderstanding in the book?

2. **Faith and conscience:** The Plain Brethren characters live by deep convictions. How did their beliefs shape their choices? Were there moments when their faith seemed at odds with survival or love?

3. **Moral courage:** What does courage look like in this story?

4. **Generational interest:** Do you feel this book appeals to multiple generations? Why or why not?

5. **Communications:** Discuss the implications of the techniques used to communicate within the book, the style of the communications, and the speed of transmission of information.

6. **Loss and remembrance:** The title *One Tragic June* suggests both a moment in time and lasting consequence. What does that title come to mean for you by the end of the book?

7. **Cultural separation:** The Plain Brethren community often stands apart from the world. Did you sympathize more with their separation or with those who question it?

8. **Historical echoes:** Did the novel make you reflect differently on how war impacts ordinary families? How might those same moral questions apply today?

9. **Historical Fiction:** Historical fiction brings light to something in the present. What was brought to light in this book?

10. **After reading:** If you could ask the author one question about the real people behind *One Tragic June*, what would it be?

—— ∞ —— ∞ —— ∞ —— ∞ —— ∞ —— ∞ —— ∞ ——

Author's Note

Jean Pugh Shipman invites readers to look beyond the tragedy and discover the resilience that history leaves behind. To connect with Jean, share your reflections, or invite her to your book club or event, visit: jeanpughshipman@gmail.com or on Facebook at bit.ly/4nRLn06

www.ingramcontent.com/pod-product-compliance
Lightning Source LLC
Chambersburg PA
CBHW021406110726
47901CB00008B/2078